★

Martha stepped back into the foyer and eased the door shut. It stuck before latching, held by friction. She set her briefcase on the foyer floor, slipped her handbag from her shoulder and leaned it against the briefcase, and then, careful not to brush her skirt against anything, stepped past the cartons. She stripped off her right glove and knelt to touch Wilma Oberfell's cheek.

She expected the skin to be cold, and so it was, but her nerve endings had not caught up with her intellect and the chill against her fingertips startled her. Her hand jerked, nudging the cold cheek, and the body rocked a bit, woodenly and all of a piece.

Her head swam. She braced her bare hand on the floor and, closing her eyes, summoned the distancing power of words. Rigor, she thought. Rigor mortis, well established.

★

"Ms. Sprague's choice of a dynamic older sleuth is inspired...an utterly engaging creation, levelheaded and compassionate..."

—*New York Law Journal*

DEATH
IN GOOD COMPANY

GRETCHEN SPRAGUE

WORLDWIDE®

TORONTO • NEW YORK • LONDON
AMSTERDAM • PARIS • SYDNEY • HAMBURG
STOCKHOLM • ATHENS • TOKYO • MILAN
MADRID • WARSAW • BUDAPEST • AUCKLAND

This story is dedicated to the departed writers:
Jennifer, who said, "You look like a lawyer,"
and Gil, who introduced me to Martha.

DEATH IN GOOD COMPANY

A Worldwide Mystery/March 1999

First published by St. Martin's Press, Incorporated.

ISBN 0-373-26303-1

Printed In U.S.A.

NOTE

The people, lawyers, places, institutions and legal procedures described in this story do not exist in what is commonly known as the "real world." The alternative universe in which they have their being bears a strong resemblance to that world, but the two are not quite identical. As a consequence, readers familiar with the real boroughs of Brooklyn and Manhattan, and with the procedures of various courts and police precincts situated therein, may find elements of this alternative universe that do not quite jibe with their experience.

In particular, West Brooklyn Legal Services is not the Legal Services office that occupies space on the real Court Street, nor have any of its staff members and clients ever walked the streets of the real Brooklyn.

ONE

THE YOUNG MAN who burst into the corner office was Latino, handsome, and—judging by the red blotches on the tissues he was pressing to his forehead—bleeding.

Howard Wallace interrupted his third repetition of, "Above all, Martha, avoid the Mother Teresa syndrome," and said instead, "Carlos. What have you done to yourself?"

The young man flicked a glance at Martha.

"You've heard of Martha Patterson," said Howard. "She is now on board. Martha, this is Carlos Quinones, one of our highly valued paralegals, who seems to have damaged himself. What happened?"

Carlos said, "I got mugged."

"Good lord," said Howard. "How did that happen?"

"Three guys with knives."

"Did you get cut?"

"Hey, Howard, I get cut, I'm getting stitched up in the emergency room. I got lucky, just scraped my head." He lifted the wad of tissues, revealing a scrape that extended from his eyebrow into his hairline. A drop of blood welled up.

Martha, having raised a child, was no stranger to bloody scrapes. This one, though doubtless painful, was far from dangerous.

The drop of blood trickled past Carlos's eyebrow toward his cheekbone.

Howard said, "Did you lose consciousness?"

Carlos refolded the tissues, dabbed at the trickle, and pressed the wad to the scrape again. "Not really. I guess I was a little woozy for a minute."

"Where did it happen?"

"In the subway. I was coming back from The Building."

Howard's venerable swivel chair rocked forward an inch. "*The* building?"

"With the rent strike. I was picking up the rent for Luther. I'm just through the turnstile, a little ways down the platform, and these guys, three guys, they pile in behind me, come up on both sides and one of them behind me, like surrounding me? With these knives."

Howard was very still.

"Like gravity knives? Flick-knives? I'm going to argue with three knives?"

Martha heard Howard draw in a breath. He held it a moment before he let it out.

"Listen," said Carlos. "I don't argue with knives. They march me down to the end, where the catwalk goes down in the tunnel? Shove me up against the wall, that's where I get this." Again he raised the wad of tissues. Another drop of blood welled up. "It's cement, you know? The wall down there? They rip off my wallet, and then they take the rent money. I was bringing it to Luther to deposit in court. In one of those portfolios, you know? With the elastic around it? They grabbed it and took off. I'm going to argue with three knives?"

Howard said, "No." He swiveled to his desk, punched digits into the phone, said, "John, your pro bono is here," and swiveled back. "No, you aren't going to argue with three knives. We're not even going to discuss knives and the proper response thereto.'' His chair came upright and he planted his hands on his knees. "We're going to back up to before the knives, and you're going to explain to me why the hell you were carrying the rent payments for an entire six-story building in one of those portfolios with an elastic around it''—he turned up the volume a notch—"*on the subway.*"

Carlos's eyes flicked to Martha and back. "My car wouldn't start.''

Howard said, "Your car wouldn't start.''

"You got it, Howard. Like you turn the key and it goes *yur-yur-yur.* What you call it is, your car won't start.''

Martha tried to imagine a paralegal's addressing the managing partner of her old firm, Reilly, Whitman, in that tone. Her mind refused the task.

But it would not do to smile. The situation was serious and Howard had his limits.

Clearly aware that he was approaching them, Carlos said, "Look, I had to get there some way. Luther deposits the rent in court today. I *tried* to find somebody in the street to give me a jump.''

"The office would pay for a cab.''

"You ever try to get a cab to go to that neighborhood? I figured I'd get McInerny to ride back with me, like an escort, you know? But he wasn't home. Look, I didn't think it'd look like I had *money* in that thing. That's the kind of thing you carry papers or something.''

Martha's peripheral vision picked up movement in the doorway. She glanced over.

John had arrived. He caught her glance and raised an eyebrow.

She repressed another smile. John Ainsworth, shortly to become her supervisor, was uncommonly decorative: fair-haired, blue-eyed, slightly built but excellently proportioned, handsomely featured, and possessed of the enviable muscle control to raise a single eyebrow.

And, in his early thirties, less than half her age. This fact would have troubled Martha more if it had seemed to trouble John at all. He stood at ease, urbane in jacket and tie, just inside the doorway.

Howard was saying, "If McInerny wasn't there, who was holding the money?"

"Wilma had it," said Carlos. "That fat old lady hangs out with McInerny? You know the one; Enid's got her case."

"The rent," Howard said. "What form was it in?"

"Money orders, a couple checks. A couple in cash."

"Ah." Howard let out a sigh. "Have you notified the tenants to stop payment?"

"Hey, gimme a break. Luther's in court, waiting for the rent, right? Soon as they took off, I got on the first train and got my ass"—he glanced at Martha, who had noticed nothing amiss until his hesitation—"got over to housing court. Then Luther says get over here and tell you. So I'm here telling you."

"Is Luther notifying the tenants?"

"He's on trial."

"Then you do it. Right away."

"Right. Sure."

"And get me a copy of the police report."

"Hey, if there was a cop to report it to, I wouldn't get mugged in the first place."

"The token clerk has radio contact."

"Yeah, well, I wasn't about to follow those brothers back to the gate. Not with three knives. And then the train came in, and what I thought was get my ass out of there, get over to court and tell Luther.''

Howard rocked backward and forward an inch.

Carlos said, "Like I said, I guess maybe I was a little woozy right about then.''

"OK. Call it in now.''

"What good's that going to do? There wasn't anybody saw what went down except them and me, and those guys are long gone.''

"No doubt. But the insurer is going to need a police report, and any tenants that may have to get an emergency grant from welfare will need a police report. Call the precinct over there and make the report. Then, right away, get the tenant list out of the file and call everybody in that building and tell them to stop payment on those checks and money orders. Then write the whole thing up and get it typed and put it in my box before you leave. And get to a doctor and find out if you've got any concussion or other damage, and bring me the doctor's report tomorrow. Got it?''

Carlos opened his mouth, obviously thought better of what he had been about to say, and closed it. He compressed the wad of bloody tissues in his fist and pitched it toward Howard's wastebasket. It hit the rim and landed on the floor. He saluted, said to the space in front of him, "Yes *sir*, General Wallace, sir,'' and wheeled toward the doorway.

John stepped aside and said, "Yo, Carlos.''

"Yo, John.'' Carlos vanished.

John picked up the tissue wad with the thumb and forefinger of his left hand, dropped it into Howard's wastebasket, turned, and with extended right hand said, "Welcome aboard, Martha.''

It was happening.

A ripple of trepidation crosshatched the waning ripples of her amusement. She said, "Thank you," rose from her chair, shook John's hand, and stepped into her role as volunteer attorney for West Brooklyn Legal Services.

TWO

Alone in John Ainsworth's office, Martha took a legal pad from her briefcase and a pen from her handbag.

Until this moment, working pro bono for West Brooklyn Legal Services, a poverty-law office providing civil legal representation to the indigent, had been largely a concept. More than a notion, certainly, but not quite a concrete reality. Now it was happening.

She had been a trusts and estates lawyer at Reilly, Whitman since 1949. That was the year in which she had received her law degree, married Edwin Patterson, and moved from Lincoln, Nebraska, to New York City, where Edwin had turned his wartime experience in the Air Corps into a promising small airfreight business. Her father, a justice of the Nebraska Supreme Court, had exercised his considerable influence to obtain her an offer from Reilly, Whitman. "I did this much," he said, kissing her good-bye after the wedding. "The rest is up to you."

The rest was now history. The firm had retired her a little over three years ago. Edwin had sold his business at an immense profit and at once suffered a series of disabling heart attacks. Martha acquired a modem and a fax and did freelance legal research out of the apartment—enough, as she put it, to keep the brain from turning to Jell-O. But when Edwin died three years later, the apartment became a prison. Martha found herself with enough money to do much as she pleased, but with little idea what it was she pleased.

She had met Howard Wallace many years before, when he had interned at Reilly, Whitman for a summer. Although their career paths had diverged, they had kept in touch. A few months after Edwin's death, she ran into him at a Bar Association dinner. When she responded honestly to his, "How are you, Martha?" he promptly offered to put her to work as a pro bono lawyer at West Brooklyn.

She said yes. He set up meetings and assigned homework; now it was happening. The office manager had issued her a set of keys, explained the coffee pool, and entered her name in the Christmas-party gift drawing. John had showed her a partly emptied utility closet that was eventually to be her office. "Somebody was supposed to clean it out, but he was interrupted by an emergency," John explained. "Standard Legal Services practice. Emergencies interrupt emergencies." As for today, Howard had left after welcoming Martha and would be out for the balance of the afternoon; Martha could camp out temporarily in his office.

John had then escorted her to his office, to which he would return in a few minutes with the rest of the Government Benefits Unit, who would hand off to her the beginnings of a caseload of her very own.

Her hands were cold. This, however, was not altogether the result of trepidation; the place was noticeably chilly.

West Brooklyn was decorated in keeping with its funding level. Previous visits had somewhat inured Martha to the wood-grain laminate that paneled the walls, the discordant vinyl floor tile, and the mud-colored industrial carpeting in Howard's corner office and in the reception area out front, where the clients waited on the cheapest of fiberglass-and-chrome chairs.

But she was not yet inured to the undisguised poverty of those clients. Her trusts-and-estates clients at Reilly, Whitman had come to her in search of hiding places where their excess might grow more excessive. Now, sitting next to John Ainsworth's hand-me-down desk, she thought that the comfort in which she so obviously lived must surely give offense to these new clients whose problems she was about to address.

Howard, however, said not. Howard said, *Above all, avoid the Mother Teresa syndrome.* The clients needed lawyers, and they wanted their lawyers to talk like lawyers, dress like lawyers, live like lawyers. West Brooklyn Legal Services was undeniably—and comfortingly—a functioning law office: telephones beeped; computer terminals hummed; in the corridor near John's office, secretaries gossiped as they shepherded a collating job through the copy machine.

At that point in Martha's meditations, John reappeared, accompanied by a slight young woman bundled in a large, frayed, faded black sweatshirt. The sleeves were turned back, and flyaway auburn hair escaped around the edge of a hood pulled to her arched eyebrows. He introduced this attractive pixie as Anita Pagan, a paralegal. "Anita taught me all I know," he said. "Ask her the hard questions."

It was evident that paralegals at West Brooklyn Legal Services were held in considerably higher esteem than were the diligent gofers at Reilly, Whitman. Martha said, "How do you do, Anita," and wrote on her legal pad: "Anita Pagan, respected paralegal. Elf."

Anita said, "Hi, Martha," and crossed to perch on the cold radiator, her hands tucked into her armpits. "This is ridiculous," she said to John. "It's three in the afternoon."

"Sixty-two." John turned his chair, sat down with his back to the desk, and said to Martha, "The contract sends them home after half an hour at fifty-five."

"The contract," said Anita, "was negotiated by gringos."

"The super," said John, "insists on turning down the thermostat over the weekend, but the heat's usually up by ten."

Anita said, "I'm going back to San Juan."

John sang, "Everything's fine in A-mer-i-ca," and then the rest of the Government Benefits Unit arrived, dragging chairs and carrying case files.

Determined not to be embarrassed by her long-standing difficulty in remembering names, Martha wrote underneath Anita's name: "Orlando Pierce, paralegal; Gwen Doherty, paralegal, disability specialist; Victory King, lawyer." A lanky black man with a tall haircut; a chunky white woman; a short, round, very young black woman.

Politically incorrect, thought Martha. Victory King should be the unit director, Orlando and Anita senior attorneys, John a highly valued paralegal. But John had introduced Victory as a rookie, just a month past the news that she had passed the New York State bar exam. Her time would surely come. And perhaps Anita and Orlando were attending law school at night. John's position was beyond remedying.

Victory said, "You hear Carlos got mugged?"

"Speed of light," said John to Martha. "Get used to it."

"Got mugged twice," said Orlando.

Gwen said, "What do you mean?"

"Got mugged in the subway and then Howard gave him hell for getting mugged."

"Not for getting mugged," said John. "For carrying the rent on the subway. Not bright."

Anita said, "John, he was hurt and they took his wallet, and all Howard did was yell at him about the rent."

"How much did he lose?" asked John. "Personally?"

"Well, he was carrying most of his money in his sock. But Howard never asked. And he was hurt."

"A scrape on his forehead. Hardly life-threatening. And Howard did tell him to go to the doctor."

"For workers' comp," said Anita. The radiator emitted three bangs and began to hiss. "I don't believe it."

"Oh, ye of little faith. No, you're right. Howard failed to overflow with compassion when he heard the rent was gone. Let's proceed, gang. Martha needs a caseload. What can we off-load on her?"

She got four cases for starters. One of them, originally Gwen's, she almost didn't get.

"Tessie Doone," said Gwen. "Wheelchair-bound, says her SSI checks stopped without warning."

John asked, "Where does she live?"

Gwen read off an address.

"Isn't that The Building?"

Martha heard implied capitalization and said, "The building with the rent strike?"

Anita nodded and John said to Gwen, "Listen; first find out if she can travel."

Martha said, "I'll go to her if she can't." Perceiving a hesitation, she said, "Or am I not to make house calls?"

After another little pause, John said, "Sorry. Give her the file, Gwen."

"Thank you," said Martha.

"If you have to go, take a car service."

AND SO IT CAME ABOUT that late on the afternoon of Monday, the fourth of December, 1995, Martha Patterson sat at the desk of the director of West Brooklyn Legal Services, drew a deep breath, picked up the phone, and punched in Tessie Doone's number.

The ringing tone buzzed five times; then, through an assault of high-volume TV, Martha heard a cracked, "Whozzat?"

She pitched her voice above the game show. "Is that Tessie Doone?"

"Wait a minute, lemme turn it down."

The TV diminished to faint squawks, and after a moment Martha heard again, "Whozzat?"

"This is Martha Patterson, from West Brooklyn—"

"You that lawyer bout my SSI?"

"Yes—"

"I don know why they stop my SSI. Vibelle's welfare don mount to nothin—Vibelle, she be my niece—an Roy Rogers don pay enough to keep nobody. If it wasn Kareem working, we all'd be in one of them shelters, and that's the truth."

"I'll be working on the SSI problem, Ms. Doone. I'll need to see you."

"I cain get out none."

"I'll come to you. How about tomorrow?"

"You comin over here? You gon have to walk up, that elevator ain workin again."

"When is a good time?"

"You better come when Kareem here. He unnerstand this stuff better'n me."

"When will he be there?"

"He start work at one."

"In the afternoon?"

"He don have to go before noon, twelve-fifteen."

Martha, a morning person from birth, said, "How about nine o'clock?"

"In the mornin?"

"Would that be all right?"

"Kareem, he don get up so early. He don go to work till one in the afternoon."

"Nine-thirty, then?"

"Well—OK. Yeah, OK. Yeah, I get him up."

"Do you have any papers from SSI?"

"I got somethin, I don know if that's what you want."

"I'll look at it. One more thing, Ms. Doone—is your building the one that is having a rent strike?"

"Ain nothin happenin. He ain even fix that elevator yet."

"But you are withholding your rent from the landlord?"

"Ain doin no good, what I can see."

"Has anybody called you this afternoon about your rent?"

"Kareem pay the rent yesterday mornin."

"Nobody called you today?"

"Call me bout what? Kareem, he give that rent over to Frank McInerny. I see him go down with it."

"No, that's not the problem. I mean after that, this afternoon. Our paralegal was mugged on the way to court, and the rent money for the building got stolen."

"Got stole?"

Movement at the doorway caught Martha's eye. As Tessie Doone's voice said in her ear, "All that there rent for the whole buildin? Got stole?" Martha's divided attention registered a heavyset white woman in a shabby tan coat. Martha gave her a nod and said into the phone, "Did you pay with a money order or a check, or did you pay cash?"

"Kareem, he payin the rent, now my SSI stop comin. If he don have no job, we be on the street."

"Did he write a check?"

"He don have no bank account. He buy a money order, that check-cashin place he go when he get his paycheck."

"He should put in a stop-payment order right away."

"They cain nobody cash a money order without it's made out to them, can they?"

"They might forge a signature. Kareem should go back to where he bought it and have payment stopped. Right away today, if you can get in touch with him."

"The boss don want him gettin calls at work."

"First thing in the morning, then. Don't worry if he isn't there when I come; it's more important to get payment stopped on that money order."

She expected another objection, but suddenly Tessie Doone acquiesced. "Yeah, OK," she said. "I tell him."

Martha hung up and turned her attention to the visitor. The woman's broad face was an unhealthy red. Graying blond hair was pulled back into a disheveled bun. Under the unbuttoned camel's hair coat she wore a maroon polyester pantsuit with pulled threads. A crammed leather tote bag hung from one arm.

Martha said, "If you're looking for Mr. Wallace, he's out of the office."

"Is Mr. Wallace the one in charge?" Two Brooklynese syllables: *chaw-awge.*

"He's—yes. He's the project director. I'm Martha Patterson. May I ask your name?"

The woman hesitated; at last she offered, "Wilma Oberfell."

Wilma. Someone had spoken that name this afternoon. Martha said, "Is there something I can do for you?"

The woman said, "I don't remember seeing you before. Are you the…the second in command?"

"No, I'm one of the lawyers. We wouldn't have met; I just started today."

"Is he coming back?"

"I believe he's gone for the day. Perhaps there's someone else you'd like to talk with."

Wilma looked over her shoulder into the corridor. Then she advanced a step, closed the door behind her, and dropped her voice. "I don't know whom I can trust."

Oh, my.

But after the initial jolt, Martha was not unduly discomposed. Four decades of trusts-and-estates practice had exposed her to a certain number of disordered personalities, and Legal Services case handlers probably tolerated even more derangement in their clients than the common run of lawyers. Meanwhile, her mind threw out the observation that the woman knew how to use *whom.*

The phone warbled. Martha swiveled back, picked up, and said, "Howard Wallace's office, Martha Patterson speaking."

John's voice said, "Do you want some backup?"

His office was just two doors up the corridor; he must have sensed that the activity in the corner office was a bit beyond the usual.

In truth, Martha doubted that she needed assistance, but perhaps this was a situation in which management should be involved. Not entirely happily, she said, "Perhaps so."

He said, "On my way." And as the phone clicked dead, the context in which she had heard the name *Wilma* clicked into her consciousness. The rent strike. Somebody named Wilma had been holding the rent—now stolen—to give to Carlos Quinones.

The woman had approached closely enough for Martha to see that she had remarkably attractive green eyes, nearly lost in the hypertensive ruddiness of her face. "I hope," she said unexpectedly, "you don't think I'm being paranoid."

As Martha was searching for an answer both truthful and prudent, a rap on the door made her jump. Wilma jerked around to look over her shoulder. The door opened and John stepped in.

Wilma said, "Oh."

John said, "Oh, hello, Ms. Oberfell. Are you looking for Enid? I think she's in court."

"Oh," said Wilma again. She turned back to Martha. "No. No, thank you. I was just"—those extraordinary green eyes insisted on making contact—"just in the neighborhood…"

Martha caught herself beginning to nod, as if accepting a confidence. As if letting herself be cast in the role of a conspirator against those who couldn't be trusted.

Madness. She broke eye contact and Wilma lapsed into silence. Then she said, "I'm sorry to have bothered you," dividing the routine apology between the two of them. "I'll call back for an appointment."

John said, "Good idea. Howard comes and goes a lot."

"Yes," said Wilma. "I understand."

And that was the anticlimactic end of it; under John's escort, Wilma plodded off up the corridor.

Martha stood and walked to a window. Four floors down, late-afternoon traffic honked up and down Court Street.

"Wilma had it," Carlos had said. "That fat old lady hangs out with McInerny? You know the one; Enid's got her case."

"I don't know whom I can trust," Wilma had said.

"Sorry about that," said John behind her. "Clients aren't supposed to be back here on their own, but now and then Gloria gets distracted."

Martha turned from the window. "You know her."

"I see her around. She's got a custody case pending in family court."

"She has a child?"

"Strange to relate. What was her problem?"

"She wanted to talk with whoever was in charge of the office."

"And found you in the hot seat. Sorry about that. What did she want to talk about?"

"She didn't say." It was too bad she had admitted John into the scene. Still, courtesy demanded that she acknowledge his readiness to ease her way. "I must thank you for the rescue."

"A pleasure," he said.

BY A FEW MINUTES PAST five, Martha had analyzed her tiny caseload, charted her course, and made her phone calls. She couldn't remember when she had last left work that early. She stopped in John's office to deposit her files and, to her surprise, found him packing his briefcase.

"All-nighter," he said. He followed her into the corridor.

Not everyone was leaving; many offices still spilled light into the corridors. But Building Maintenance was ending its day; a wheeled trash barrel stood just inside the door to the waiting room. Martha took her coat from a row of hooks next to the door and saw that Anita Pagan had hung her tatty old sweatshirt on the hook next to it.

John set his briefcase on the floor and held the coat for her. "You'd better leave it in my office until you get a room of your own," he said. Martha looked over her shoulder at him and he tilted his head toward the waiting room. "Most of them wouldn't, but it isn't fair to dangle temptation."

"Oh," she said. "Just so. Thank you."

Out in the waiting room, the switchboard was dark, the receptionist's chair was tucked into the kneehole of her desk, and a cleaning woman was shoving chairs together at one end of the waiting room. In the middle of the cleared space, Carlos Quinones and a lawyer from the Landlord-Tenant Unit stood with an obviously anxious couple, the lawyer rustling through a sheaf of blue-backed papers, Carlos translating.

John punched the elevator button.

Martha said, "You work at home rather than here?"

"It gets spooky," he said. "There isn't any night porter. The building pretty much empties out by seven or eight. Except for Howard. He's been known to put in some late hours." The elevator slid open and discharged a tall woman carrying a briefcase. John said, "Hello, Enid."

She said, "Hello, John," but her eyes were on Martha.

"Martha Patterson," John said, "this is Enid Morgan."

"Martha." Enid offered her hand. She was a good-looking woman, tall and dark-haired, with strong bones and olive skin. Martha returned her handshake.

"Wilma Oberfell was in," said John.

The level dark eyebrows rose. "What did she want?"

"To me, she did not utter. She got past the front desk and went back to Howard's office, but he wasn't here and she drew Martha instead."

Enid looked at Martha, who said, "She wanted to talk to the person in charge of the office. I told her he was out, and then John came by and took her away." She hesitated; some of that odd sense of complicity lurked. But that was madness. The woman, after all, was Enid's client. "She said she didn't know whom to trust."

"Trust?" For a moment, Enid's face lost all expression. Then she said, "Damn."

"Is this something you understand?"

"She's scheduled for a court-ordered psychiatric tonight. Just the time for a paranoid outburst."

Martha had more than once sat behind one-way glass to observe court-ordered psychiatric examinations. "Is she given to such things?"

"She can be seriously weird. Thanks for the warning."

"You're quite welcome," said Martha, and stepped into the elevator.

Following her, John said over his shoulder, "Have

fun,'' and as the space narrowed, Martha heard Enid say, "Thank you, John."

It was not an amiable exchange. Enid's last words, in fact, had sounded very much like "Fuck you, John."

Hm.

Martha said, "What is this all-nighter you're undertaking?"

"Preliminary injunction motion and motion for class determination. Eastern District."

A federal case. Serious litigation. "What's your issue?"

"A challenge to a long-standing practice we call churning. Constantly deplored, never remedied. People keep getting bumped off the welfare rolls for paperwork reasons that have nothing to do with need. I'm trying to stitch together a legal theory out of rags and patches."

"It sounds challenging."

"Howard's word is quixotic, but he gives people rope. And since the practice lands families in shelters, which are expensive, there's some political appeal to the budget balancers."

"Will the restrictions on class actions that Congress is proposing cause you any trouble?"

"Bound to. We'll carry it as far as we can, and if push comes to shove we'll farm it out to the private bar."

"When you've patched together your argument, I'd be interested to see it. If you wouldn't mind."

"Mind? Surely you jest. The more heads, the better." The elevator lurched to a stop and the door began to open. "Oh, shit," he said, and then, quickly, "Sorry."

"You've forgotten something."

"A crucial reference. I have to go back up."

"At least," she said, "you haven't got all the way home."

MOUNTING THE STEPS in front of her building, Martha found herself gazing as if with a client's eyes through the glass walls of the lobby at the aesthetically agreeable sofa and easy chair located at a discreet distance beyond the doorman's podium and the healthy little indoor grove of ficus trees that screened the mailboxes and the elevators.

It undoubtedly bore little resemblance to The Building.

She pushed through the door and uttered her routine, "Good evening," to Boris, the evening doorman, whom she rather disliked. Avoiding eye contact, she glanced past him at the little slice of street visible through the glass wall. Her eyes fell on a disheveled figure standing at the foot of the entrance steps.

Wilma Oberfell.

Wilma Oberfell?

Oh, surely not. Surely this was an optical illusion, conjured up by a sense of unfinished business—her warned-against Mother Teresa syndrome manufacturing a familiar, disturbing figure out of a casual passerby. She stepped past Boris for a better view.

Bulky body in shabby camel's hair coat, red face, straggling bun, tote bag—it was the veritable Wilma Oberfell.

An impulse twitched at Martha, to turn back, go out, accost the woman, hear her out—

But as she teetered between urge and resistance, Wilma Oberfell—yes, it really was Wilma—turned and lumbered off, passing rapidly out of sight.

THREE

THE CAR SERVICE DRIVER looked back over his shoulder and said, "This address you give, is right?"

Thirty years before, the question would have been incomprehensible. This area of Flatbush had been middle-class; Martha and Edwin Patterson had more than once been entertained at dinner only a couple of blocks from where Martha now peered out at a ribby dog sniffing at a pile of leaking garbage bags beside a burned-out car.

Feeling as alien as if she had green skin and antenna ears, Martha said, "Yes, don't worry. Keep going."

And, yes, a block farther along, tarnished gilt numbers on a dirty fanlight over the double front doors of a six-story brick apartment building displayed the address she was looking for.

The Building.

Graffiti-blotched plywood was tacked over the spaces in the front door where beveled glass panes had once looked out on the street.

The uneasiness in her midsection was two steps beyond trepidation.

She looked at her watch. She had calculated the time of the trip accurately; it was just past nine.

She handed over the fare and a substantial tip, thrust her billfold deep into her handbag and zipped the compartment closed, shoved the door open, and emerged nearly into the path of a young black woman pushing a bundled baby in a stroller and towing a toddler by the wrist.

"I beg your pardon," said Martha.

The young woman said, "OK," and veered past her.

An elderly couple strolling arm in arm responded to Martha's nervous smile with smiles of their own. Three young men, conversing in a loud argot of which every third word seemed to be *man,* gave her concerted stares as they passed; it might have been hostile; it might have been curious; it might have been simply habitual.

She crossed the sidewalk, pulled open the front door, stepped through into the vestibule, and let the door swing closed behind her. The smell would not have been out of place in a back alley in Naples. She breathed shallowly and managed not to gag. In front of her, the inner door was missing; the lobby beyond was empty.

In the vestibule, a bare bulb in a broken fixture gave off just enough light to let her read the names slotted in the panel of bell pushes. Fewer than half of the slots held names. A barely legible DOONE was penciled on a grimy slip of paper beside 3-C. That would be her client.

OBERFELL appeared in raised print on a scissored-off fragment of business card in the 4-F slot. She would be surprised to find a working intercom, but for form's sake she pressed the button. On another sliver, next to 2-F, she noticed FRANCIS X. MCINERNY.

There was no answering buzz from 4-F.

The lobby was floored with grimy hexagonal tiles that had once been white. In there the smell was not so strong and the light was better. Mailboxes were inset into one wall. Several of their doors were sprung and bulging; one dangled on a twisted hinge. On the elevator door at the rear of the lobby, she could just make out the words OUT OF ODER penciled in uneven capitals on a folded brown paper bag.

But dilapidated though it might be, the building was by no means derelict. Voices seeped through apartment doors, mingled with the muted din of daytime television. Somewhere higher up a door slammed; Martha heard young female voices and the shuffle-slap of shoe soles on the stairs.

The inner stair rail had broken from the bolts that held it to the wall and was resting on the steps. But the outer banister felt solid enough under her gloved hand, and she started up. Something had been spilled; her right shoe sole stuck slightly on each step. She met the descending girls—three of them, in their midteens, with book packs over their shoulders and uniform plaid skirts showing below their jackets—between the first and second floors. One of them said, "You lookin' for Aunt Tessie?"

"Tessie Doone?" said Martha.

The girl said, "Three-C," jerking her head upward.

Martha said, "Thank you," and the girl smiled and pattered on down the stairs after her companions.

Above the second floor, Martha could breathe normally. Either altitude was attenuating the smell or her olfactory nerves had shut down. She paused to scuff her right sole on the edge of one step and got rid of most of the stickiness. She did not stop on the third floor but turned and mounted the next flight. On the landing between the third and fourth floors she paused to catch her breath and look at her watch. Seven minutes past nine. Were the girls going to be late for school? Perhaps even parochial schools were on staggered sessions these days.

The light fixture on the fourth floor was missing its bulb. Daylight crept through a dirty window beside the head of the stairs and a little more light leaked down from the landing above, but there was little illumination on the door of Apartment 4-F when she found it tucked behind the staircase. OBERFELL, on another sliver of card under the bell push, was barely decipherable.

She pressed the bell push. She couldn't hear whether the doorbell rang. She waited, pressed the button again, waited again. Finally she knocked.

The door gave way under her gloved knuckles and swung a couple of inches inward, and a chilly breeze brushed her face. She heard the quiet chatter of television. She pressed the bell push again and now she could hear a soft *ding-dong*. The *ding* was cracked, the *dong* clear.

Nobody answered. Pitching her voice over the television's soft babble, she called out, "Hello?"

No answer.

"Ms. Oberfell? Wilma? Hello!"

Just the babble.

She pushed the door in a few inches farther, revealing a tiny foyer and a crowd of furniture in the room beyond.

"Hello!" she called again.

Only the electronic chitter-chatter.

She opened the door wide and took a step into the foyer. What she could see of the room beyond was chockablock—massive easy chairs, a matching sofa, side tables covered with geegaws, a shelf system crammed with books and cartons. More cartons were stacked head-high around the walls. The breeze swept past her into the hall; she heard a hissing radiator battling the chill.

"Hello!" she called. "Wilma!"

Only the TV.

Another step brought the right half of the apartment into view. An open rollaway bed stood against the far wall; a faded flowered sheet and a matching comforter were rumpled and thrown back. A ten-inch television on a brass-wire stand at the foot of the bed was tuned to a public-television children's program, hand puppets and chirpy voices. The left-hand end of the room was still blocked by a stack of cartons. One more step brought her past them.

Her heart gave a violent thud and leaped into a gallop.

Somebody was lying on the floor.

Where the scuffed linoleum of the kitchen area gave way to scuffed floorboards, a woman was lying faceup, arms and legs splayed out. Her face was a horror. The tongue protruded, forcing apart lips that were nearly black—as if, commented Martha's unruly mind, the woman had been sucking on a leaky ballpoint. The skin was blue-white. Startling green eyes bulged, wide-open and glassy, staring sightlessly at the ceiling.

Wilma.

Martha reached out to the nearest stack of cartons for support. Nausea thrust against the back of her throat. She clamped her tongue to the roof of her mouth until it subsided.

The gray-blond hair, released from its daytime bun, straggled onto the floor. A flannel nightgown sprigged with faded pink rosebuds, the surface pilled with laundering, was rucked halfway up pallid fat-dimpled thighs.

Across the room, the puppets were chirping a song.

Martha stepped back into the foyer and eased the

door shut. It stuck before latching, held by friction. She set her briefcase on the foyer floor, slipped her handbag from her shoulder and leaned it against the briefcase, and then, careful not to brush her skirt against anything, stepped past the cartons. She stripped off her right glove and knelt to touch Wilma Oberfell's cheek.

She expected the skin to be cold, and so it was, but her nerve endings had not caught up with her intellect and the chill against her fingertips startled her. Her hand jerked, nudging the cold cheek, and the body rocked a bit, woodenly and all of a piece.

Her head swam. She braced her bare hand on the floor and, closing her eyes, summoned the distancing power of words. *Rigor,* she thought. *Rigor mortis, well established.*

The faintness ebbed. She pushed herself to her feet. Working her glove back over her fingers, she scanned the cluttered apartment for a telephone, finding it at last on a shelf at the head of the bed, an ivory-colored dial model. With a fine tremor vibrating through her muscles, she lifted the phone with the tips of her gloved left fingers and with her gloved right index finger dialed 911.

One of the puppets was telling a joke.

FOUR

DETECTIVE VERA JAMISON closed her notebook. Martha looked at her watch. Somehow, while she had been telling everything she knew about Wilma Oberfell, it had got to be nearly ten-thirty.

After she had called 911, she had called Tessie Doone. "I'm sorry, I'm going to be late," she had said.

"I ain goin nowhere," Tessie's cracked voice had responded through the blare of television.

Presently two uniformed patrolmen had thumped up the stairs, Martha opening the door for them in what felt like an absurd, hostessly gesture. The detectives arrived a quarter of an hour later. Detective Dominick DiAngelo was a stocky man with a square, hook-nosed face; Detective Vera Jamison was a thin copperskinned woman with copper-colored hair worn close to her well-shaped head in cornrows. Martha repeated the names aloud: "Dominick DiAngelo. Vera Jamison."

It was Detective Jamison who took Martha's statement, down in the backseat of the unmarked car. Through the windows Martha could see the shifting mélange of faces behind the police barrier. At intervals the radio in the front seat punctuated her narrative with indecipherable squawks of which Detective Jamison took no notice.

At one point, a blue-and-white NYPD van pulled to the curb in front of them. Martha watched two men in plain clothes get out. One stood for several minutes with his hands in his pockets, looking at the entrance to The Building; the other unloaded things from the rear of the van.

Crime-scene experts, she thought. Fingerprints, photographs, measurements; the collection of fibers and alien flecks of dust and traces of body fluids—

A fine tremor affected her voice for a moment. After a while she saw them go into The Building.

Now she peered out at the patrolman who was holding back the curious behind sawhorses and yellow tapes. "Will the officer let me in?" she asked.

Detective Jamison's eyebrows arched.

"I still need to interview my client," said Martha.

"Well now, you've had a rough morning, Ms. Patterson," said Detective Jamison. "Maybe you ought to go home and relax."

Go home? In the middle of a workday? With a task undone?

But of course it wasn't concern for Martha's well-being that motivated Detective Jamison. She had a homicide to investigate.

And Martha had a client to interview. She pushed the most potent button available to her. "This client has just lost almost one-third of her household income," she said. "If the matter doesn't get settled immediately, she could be at risk of homelessness."

Detective Jamison said, "We have to talk to everybody in the building."

Martha heard an imperfectly concealed hesitancy. "Just so," she said. "And I imagine Ms. Doone would feel more cooperative if she felt the police weren't standing in the way of straightening out this problem."

For a moment Detective Jamison's teeth worried at her lower lip. Then she got out of the car and closed the door behind her. Standing on the curb, she unhooked a radio from her belt. Martha watched her speak, listen, speak again. Then she replaced the walkie-talkie on her belt, twitched her loose-fitting short coat to hang freely, and opened the door. "I'll take you up," she said. She waited while Martha climbed out, slammed the door, spoke briefly to the patrolman on the sidewalk, and preceded Martha into The Building.

A knot of tenants—two or three old men, a couple of middle-aged women, a heavy young woman with a baby on her shoulder—were gathered in front of the mailboxes. Their overlapping voices hushed as Martha and Detective Jamison came in, and Martha felt their eyes on her back as she followed Detective Jamison up the stairs. On the second floor, two women stood talking in a doorway; on the next flight up, a young man with dreadlocks, descending in quick time, craned his neck to stare back up at the fourth floor before shifting his gaze to Martha and Detective Jamison.

Apartment 3-C was just at the head of the stairs. Through the closed door Martha could hear the television and a heavy beat that was more a vibration in the solar plexus than a sound.

Detective Jamison moved in front of Martha, pulling a small leather folder from her pocket with one hand; with the other she rang the bell.

Something rattled low down on the door. Martha looked down and saw a peephole set at a little above waist level. Tessie Doone's, "Whozzat?" penetrated the competing noise.

Detective Jamison bent to bring her face to the level of the peephole and flipped the folder open to bring the shield into view. "I'm a police officer, Miz Doone," dragging out the Z, turning the form of address into the southern Miz. "Detective Vera Jamison. Just need to talk to you a minute."

"What you want?"

"There's been a little trouble upstairs. I need—"

"I don have nothin to do with upstairs."

"Then it won't take long. All I want is just to ask you a couple questions. Not just you, ma'am. We have to talk to everybody in the building."

"I don know nothin bout upstairs. I cain get upstairs, I cain get nowhere without no elevator workin."

"You don't know anything, we get it over and no more hassle. Let's get it over."

"Whozzat back there?"

Detective Jamison straightened and looked at Martha.

Martha stepped past her and bent to bring her face within the scope of the peephole. "Martha Patterson, Ms. Doone. Your lawyer from West Brooklyn."

For a moment, Martha heard nothing but the TV and the heavy bass beat; then Tessie Doone said, "I don talk to no p'lice without my lawyer be here."

Martha was aware that her spirits were rising inordinately. She must watch herself; shock had put her emotions on a hairtrigger. Struggling to keep from betraying her untimely amusement, she straightened and exchanged a glance with Detective Jamison. "It's her right," she said.

"I *know.*" In the sharpened tone, Martha heard a familiar, exasperated *Lawyers!* Detective Jamison bent once more. "All right, Miz Doone."

FIVE

DETECTIVE JAMISON ENTERED first. Following her, Martha had her first glimpse of her client.

From the voice, she had expected a wrinkled crone, but Tessie Doone's face, plump and chocolate brown, was no older than late fifties. A red cable-stitch cardigan strained at its buttons over a matronly bosom. The wheelchair's leg rests supported shrunken sticks inside navy blue polyester pants.

The electronic beat was coming from farther back in the apartment.

Tessie Doone backed the wheelchair around and rolled into the living room. Martha saw Detective Jamison cast a rapid glance through a doorway into the kitchen before moving on, and stop for another scan where the foyer opened into the living room.

The room gave off a thrift-shop aura. A chipped chrome-and-Formica dinette set stood against the near wall; two easy chairs and a sofa, matching only in shabbiness, faced the TV in the farthest corner of the room. Scuffed hardwood flooring showed beyond the edges of a threadbare Oriental-patterned rug.

The pervasive beat emanated from a hallway on the far side of the living room that led to the rear of the apartment. Tessie rolled to the television and turned the sound down to a whisper, and the beat took over. She waved her hand toward the sofa. "You-all set."

Martha sat. Beneath a loose cushion, the sofa was unexpectedly hard.

Not sitting, Detective Jamison said, "Somebody else here?"

"Jus my grandson," said Tessie.

"What's his name?"

"He didn do nothin."

"I didn't say he did, Ms. Doone. I just like to know who I'm visiting."

"Kareem," said Tessie.

"Kareem Doone?"

"Hewitt. My oldest girl marry a man name Hewitt. Kareem didn do nothin. He got him a good job, full-time. Evenin shif. He go to work one o'clock, he work to eight, nine at night."

Kareem was supposed to have been at the check-cashing place the moment it opened this morning, stopping payment on the stolen money order.

"A minute," Detective Jamison said. She moved quickly back through the foyer and out of the apartment, bracing the door open with one foot. Martha heard her quiet voice out in the hall.

Tessie Doone looked at Martha and said, "You see she do Miranda an all that stuff, right?"

Miranda warning? Dear me. Martha summoned her rudimentary knowledge of criminal procedure. "You only need a Miranda warning if you get arrested."

"I didn do nothin," said Tessie. "You gon look out for me."

"Well, I'm your lawyer, Ms. Doone, but I'm not a criminal defense—"

But Tessie was shaking her head. "I didn do nothing. You jus see this p'lice lady don—"

Footsteps cut her off. Detective Jamison came back through the foyer. The other one, the man with the Italian name, was just behind her.

"Miz Doone," Vera said, "this is Detective Di-Angelo."

Tessie said, "Two a you?"

Detective DiAngelo displayed his shield. "Good morning, Ms. Doone."

Tessie said, "I didn do nothin."

"Nobody said you did."

"Kareem neither. Vibelle neither. She gone to school; she don know nothin."

"Nobody says you did. But somebody did something, so we've got to talk to all the tenants, find out if anybody knows what went down. I understand your grandson's at home."

"Kareem gotta go to work."

"I won't hold him up long. You want to call him out here, or is it all right if I go back there?"

After a moment, Tessie Doone put her hands on the wheelchair wheels. "I go get him."

"Fine."

Tessie rolled herself across the living room and swiveled the wheelchair into the hall. The two detectives stood clear, watching her back. Waiting, Martha fixed her attention on prideful little details: a flight of plaster ducks, the gilt tarnished and chips showing white along the edges of the wings, hanging on one wall; a souvenir ashtray from Disney World and the Empire State Building in a snowstorm paperweight with an air bubble at the top on the table at her elbow. Framed photographs were everywhere: a smiling boy of about twelve in a blue cap and gown, a little girl in a red dress on Santa's lap, a wedding party, a newborn in the hospital-gowned arms of a girl who looked no more than sixteen—

Down the back hall, the beat ballooned. Martha

heard voices; then the sound died and Tessie rolled into sight again. A young man followed, zipping up a denim jacket above jeans so new they showed a crease.

Kareem Hewitt was not very tall, but the jacket sleeves were snug over his biceps. His face was expressionless. His lofty mat of hair was cut straight up with designs shaved into the sides. Three gold loops were spaced up one ear. "What's the problem here?" he said.

"No problem here." Detective DiAngelo showed his shield. "There is a little problem upstairs, and we're going to have to talk to all the tenants. Not real exciting, but that's our routine."

"I got a job to get to," said Kareem.

"I understand and I don't want to interfere. So maybe we could just talk for a few minutes downstairs, and then you can cut out and do what you've got to do."

Kareem looked him over for a moment. Then he jerked his head toward the door and said, "Let's go."

Tessie closed the front door behind them and rolled herself back to her station in front of the television. "OK p'lice lady," she said, "you jus tell me now, what happen, you gotta go hasslin me an Kareem?"

Detective Jamison selected a chair from the dinette set and placed it at the angle where the foyer joined the living room. "Do you know Wilma Oberfell, Miz Doone?"

"Wilma?" Tessie rubbed one hand back and forth on the armrest. "Well—not like *knowin*. Not like comin in an settin. I know her name, like she know my name. Elevator stop workin, she pick up a loaf a bread for me, bring me my mail when she pick up hers, like that. What happen with Wilma?"

"Wilma Oberfell is dead."

Tessie looked at Martha. "How she get dead?"

Vera Jamison said, "We don't know yet."

"Gotta be somebody kill her," said Tessie Doone. "You-all don come around if it ain somebody kill her."

"We won't know until the medical examiner gets finished." Detective Jamison took out her notebook. "Just need to get a couple things straight. Tessie Doone. Is that *d-o-o-n-e?*"

"We didn do nothin."

"Nobody's saying you did, Tessie."

"What you-all here for, you don think we done somethin?"

"Come on, Tessie. Somebody gets killed in a building, we have to talk to everybody."

"Now you sayin somebody done kill her."

"We've got to act like it until we find out different."

Tessie's plump hands kneaded each other in her lap. "Wherebouts they done kill her?"

"She was found in her apartment."

"How they get in?"

"We have to find that out. We catch who it was, you can stop worrying about him getting in here."

A moment passed. Tessie sighed. "That's how you spell it."

"And you live here, in this apartment."

"I surely ain goin noplace else."

"Were you home last night?"

"Surely was."

"Did you see or hear anything unusual last night?"

"Las night. Well, now. Las night I hear her comin home. Wilma. If that's what you mean."

"When was that?"

"Well, now. Lemme think."

"After dark?"

"Oh, yeah, nighttime. Lemme think."

"Were you watching television? What was on?"

"Oh, yeah. It was the news jus coming on."

"What news do you watch?"

"Channel Nine. News jus comin on, I hear her downstairs talking to Mr. McInerny."

"McInerny?"

"Frank McInerny down in 2-F."

"You heard them talking in his apartment down on the second floor?"

"Not *in*. They was out in the hall, standin in his door."

"Were they talking loud?"

"How you mean, loud?"

"You heard them in here with the TV on?"

"Well, the TV wasn on too loud."

"Still, that's one floor down."

"Well…" Tessie shifted her weight in the wheelchair. "I be settin over by the door." The plump fingers kneaded one another. "See, I be thinkin see, Kareem, like I tole you, he work a late shif at a printin shop, like he don get off till maybe nine or ten if a late job come in. I be thinkin—Kareem maybe comin in purty soon, I take off the locks, let him in, you know?"

"He doesn't have a key?"

"Oh, sure, he got keys, but—he be my grandson, see. He be havin some hard times before, I wanna make sure he know he be, you know, welcome. Here with me. I like to let him in, he come home nights."

"What do you mean, hard times?"

"Well—I guess you find out, you bein p'lice. You got them computers tell you evthing. Kareem, he do some time upstate. He on parole now, he got this job at the printin shop, an he be stayin here with me, but it was a hard time there.''

"What was he in for?"

"They start in callin it arm robbery, but he don go up for that. He turn himsef aroun up there, they give him parole. He straight now, he didn do nothin to Wilma. He don hardly know her. Wasn but jus me an Vibelle here, them two goin on down there. Vibelle— that's my niece—she live here with me, an she asleep back in the bedroom; she don know nothin neither.''

"Where's Vibelle now?''

"School.''

"So you were out in the foyer by the door?''

"That's right.''

"With the TV turned down.''

"That's right.''

"You know, Tessie,'' said Detective Jamison, "if I heard something going down that was loud enough to hear from the second floor up here on the third floor, I'd wonder what was happening. I'd probably open the door a crack, find out if there's a problem or something.''

A pause. "I guess maybe I did, a little bit.''

"Only natural. What were they talking about?''

"All I hear, she want to go in and he ain lettin her in.''

"Go in? To his apartment?''

"Well—I ain sayin they's somethin goin on if it ain, you know what I mean. Mr. McInerny, he be a lawyer, useta be. I don want to say nothin ain so.''

"Mm-hm.''

"But—you know. Sometimes she be in there a lot. An then they's other times he don want her aroun.

What I hear, it depen on how much he put away, you know what I mean.''

''Put away?''

''Oh, he hit the bottle, like they say. Mr. McInerny, they say he useta be a lawyer, till the bottle get him and he lose his license. That's what I hear, anyhow.''

''And he and Wilma Oberfell had a relationship?''

''Well, I don want to say nothin ain so. All I say, far's I know, they know one nother pretty good. They both bein white folks, y'know, only ones in the buildin. Sometimes she be down in 2-F all day an seem like all night. An sometimes not. Las night, I guess when she come knockin on the door, he don want her aroun. They goin at it purty good, then he slam the door.''

''Did you hear him make any threats?''

''Like he gon kill her, you mean? Nothin like that. He jus saying no, he ain lettin her in, then he slam the door, an she come on upstairs.''

''Did you hear her come upstairs?''

''I *seen* her come upstairs.''

''You still had the door open, looking out?''

''No. Mr. McInerny slam his door, I don wan her thinkin I be snoopin. I shut the door, look out the peephole there. Kareem, before he go away upstate, he put that peephole in, down where I kin see.''

''And what was it you saw?''

''Jus Wilma. She come up the stairs an turn round like she goin right on up to the fourth floor.''

''Was anybody with her?''

''No, she all by herself. Ain nobody comin up with her. She come up the stairs, an she was surely a-puffin. She don carry her weight too good. An she get up there, she shut her door.''

''You heard her door shut?''

"That ain somethin you gon miss, Wilma shuttin her door. That's one a the things she be after the landlord bout, this rent strike. That door, you don slam it hard, it don catch."

"And you heard her slam it hard?"

"Yes, ma'am. Wilma slam her door when she get home las night, an that's the las I know bout her till you come in here jus now an tell me she layin up there dead an somebody maybe kill her."

"So first you heard them arguing downstairs, then Mr. McInerny slammed his door, then you saw Wilma come upstairs and you heard *her* door slam?"

"That's what happen."

"What was she wearing?"

"Her good coat. She got a black coat better'n that old tan one—camel hair, I guess they call it, with a fur collar on it. Ain that cold las night—not for December, but I guess she like that coat."

"Was she carrying anything?"

"Carryin? Like what?"

"Anything at all."

"Nothin but that big ol bag she always got. Big ol leather thing."

"How big?"

Tessie gestured. Very likely it was the bag Martha had seen Wilma carrying.

"Anything else?"

"Not that I see. Look, Miz P'lice Lady, I done tole you evthing I know. Now you gon let me talk to my lawyer bout why they ain sendin me my SSI no more?"

"Just a little more. You know anything about any relatives she had? Parents, brothers, sisters?"

"Well, they's her sister, keepin the little girl. Wilma,

she be goin to court, tryin get the little girl back from livin with her sister. That's all I know."

"She had a little girl?"

"Two, three years old, like that." Tessie looked at Martha. "She got a lawyer, that place you workin, tryin get her little girl back."

"Is there a husband?" asked Detective Jamison.

"Not no more, they ain. He die, while back. They was divorce, Wilma say. An now I done tole you evthing I know bout Wilma, you get busy findin out who kill her, an me an my lawyer here gon find out what they doin with my SSI."

AS SOON AS Detective Jamison had taken herself off, Martha addressed the subject that had nagged at her from the moment of her entry into the apartment. "The money order for the rent," she said to Tessie. "Has Kareem—"

"He goin firs thing," Tessie said. "Put in that stop like you say. Soon's they stop hasslin him."

"It's important."

"I tell him that, twice over. Soon's that detective turn him loose, he goin."

Still dubious, but powerless to carry the matter further, Martha said, "Very well," and settled into the familiar routine of fitting the disorder of human reality into the rigid framework of the law.

Tessie produced a rumpled notice from the Social Security Administration that announced, in a condescending meld of bureaucratese-trying-to-be-English, the discontinuance of Tessie Doone's SSI grant because she had resources in excess of the eligibility level. It was dated in mid-October.

"Do you know what this resource is that they're talking about?" Martha asked.

"I ain got no *re*source. Ain nothin but my SSI, an Vibelle's welfare an that little bit she make at Roy Rogers, and Kareem workin."

"Could there be a bank account somewhere you forgot about?"

"I got a bank account, I ain *forgettin* about it."

"An old Christmas Club? Did you ever buy any government bonds or something like that?"

"I ain never had nuff for that kinda thing."

"Did you ever have a job, or have you been disabled all your life?"

"Oh, I had jobs aplenty. I done domestic all my life, up till five years back, I get this disease in my spine so my legs don work no more. So they put me on SSI."

"You aren't getting Social Security?"

"Domestic, it all off the books, you know, so they don take nothin off your pay. I tell my ladies I need all my pay, don need the guvment takin none out."

"Did your employers ever give you a bonus, something like stocks or bonds?"

Tessie laughed. "I wouldn know what one a them look like. With helpin my mama and little brothers an sisters, an then the three children a my own an the granchildun long with that, my pay be jus bout what it take to live on. My ladies give me a Christmas present, I put it right out for Christmas presents for evbody else."

The front door opened and closed, and Kareem came through the foyer into the living room. As soon as he saw Martha, his face became as still as a sleeping child's.

"This my lawyer," said Tessie. "She gettin my SSI back."

Kareem's face relaxed. He bobbed his head to Martha and said, "H'lo."

Tessie said, "She say that SSI, maybe they think I got a bank account. I don know bout no bank account, do you?"

"You tell her about that money in Philadelphia?" His conversational voice was a light baritone, surprisingly pleasant. "That account Cousin Kevin put your name on?"

"That ain mine, that Kevin's money."

"It got your name on it, don't it?"

"But it ain mine. Kevin jus put my name on so if anything happen to him, I get the money. But ain nothin happen to Kevin."

Martha said, "Who is Kevin?"

"Gran's cousin," said Kareem. "Kevin Hill. He lives in Philadelphia. He got hurt in a car accident three, four years ago, and his lawyer got him a settlement. So he put it in the bank, and put Gran's name on it too, so if he died first, she'd get the money."

"We was real close," said Tessie. "Like twins, we was, when we was little kids in South Carolina. Kevin, he don never get married, so he want me to get his money if he pass first. But that ain my money. Where they get to, callin it a resource?"

Martha said, "If your name is on the account as a joint depositor, you're legally entitled to everything in there."

"But I cain take none out. It ain mine."

"How much is in the account?"

Tessie looked at Kareem. Kareem shrugged.

"Do you have the bankbook?"

Tessie looked at Kareem again. "Kevin got it, don he?" She looked back at Martha. "You tellin me they stop my SSI cause my cousin in Philadelphia put my name on his bank account? I cain pay my rent with Kevin's money."

Kareem said, "If Kevin takes her name off, will that get her back on SSI?"

"Probably," said Martha.

"Well, we better tell him to take your name off," said Kareem to Tessie.

Martha said, "We should ask for a hearing, too. We should be able to get them to restore the money they already withheld."

Kareem said, "Like go to court?"

"Something like that but not as formal. It's called an administrative hearing."

Tessie looked at Kareem. He said, "That sounds OK."

"We'll need your cousin to testify that all the money is his," said Martha, "and that he never intended Tessie to have it unless he died."

Tessie said, "He gotta come to court?"

Kareem said, "What if he write a letter saying that? Would that fix it?"

Martha said, "It would be better if he could come and testify in person."

Kareem laughed. "No way he can do that."

"He a sick old man," Tessie said.

Kareem said, "You say it ain't as formal as court. Wouldn't a letter be OK?"

Reluctantly, Martha said, "A letter would be admissible. If nothing came out at the hearing to prove otherwise, the judge should accept a letter."

"So we get Cousin Kevin to write a letter, OK?"

"And it should be notarized. Signed under oath."

"You tell me what he should say, I'll tell him," said Kareem.

SIX

MARTHA RODE BACK to West Brooklyn Legal Services with the sense of dislocation that accompanies a return from the abnormal to the quotidian. Up on the fourth floor, the receptionist greeted her as if she belonged—as, of course, she did.

It occurred to her to wonder if her office was ready. She headed down the corridor toward the utility closet next to the men's room. The route led past John Ainsworth's office. He was at his desk, his head supported by an elbow propped among law books, a pen moving across a yellow legal pad. In offices farther up the hall, the elfin Anita was interviewing a client and Gwen Doherty was poring over some papers. Orlando Pierce was out; Martha had seen his name on the sign-out sheet; his destination looked like "FH." Victory King, telephone to her ear, was gazing out her office door; she waved.

Someone had been busy. The closet was emptied of junk and seemed to have been wet-mopped; a single-pedestal desk and a two-drawer filing cabinet stood side by side against the only wall that would accommodate them; a small swivel chair had been rolled into the kneehole. A telephone stood on the desk, a client chair was tucked into a corner, and daylight entered through the single window.

Martha rolled out the chair and sat. It was adequately comfortable. A rip in the fake-leather upholstery on one armrest had been neatly patched with plastic tape. She lifted the phone; the dial tone hummed. Someone had even installed a coat hook on the back of the door. She hung up her coat and went in search of Enid Morgan.

The Family Law Unit occupied the rear of the office, down a long side corridor and around a right-angled turn. Martha found Enid in her office halfway along, telephone clamped to her ear, scribbling on a yellow pad. She looked up as Martha peered in. Martha gestured toward the client chair beside the desk; Enid nodded and waved her in.

As Martha lowered herself into the chair, the fine tremor that had been coming and going all morning once more assailed her. She clasped her hands over the top of her handbag, closed her eyes, and practiced deep breathing.

Enid was saying into the phone, "You have the directions to the shelter, right? Are the kids with you? OK. Take them and go. Don't go back home for anything.... Well, sure, I mean as soon as they discharge you.... Tina, I know it's a long way away. That's the point." She looked at Martha with a shrug, and once more Martha thought what an attractive woman she was. She radiated energy. Martha noted a gym bag in a corner beside the filing cabinet.

Enid said into the phone, "Well, whatever you decide to do, call me back. He violated the order of protection, so at least we can get him in front of the judge.... Well, you never know.... Listen, Tina, take care of yourself; take care of the kids; next time.... OK, maybe not. But call me.... Right. Bye." She cradled the phone with force. "The hell of it is, she's probably right. The bastards seem to find their darling punching bags no matter where they go. I'd tell her to get a gun, but it's specifically against policy." She pushed the telephone away. "What's up?"

One more deep breath. "I take it the police haven't contacted you yet."

"Police? About what?"

"I thought they might have called you by now. Wilma—" The unreality of the whole thing stopped her for a moment. "Wilma Oberfell is dead."

"What? My *God*. How did you—what happened?"

"Somebody—it looks as if somebody strangled her."

"My God. How did you find out?"

"I was just at The Building."

"The—you mean where she *lives*?"

"I had an appointment to interview a disabled client." The discipline of forming sentences was calming her. "I told you Wilma was in here yesterday with a story about looking for somebody to trust."

Enid nodded.

"But what I haven't had a chance to tell you is that apparently she followed me home."

"She—*followed* you? Are you serious?"

"I saw her outside my building when I got home."

"Did she talk to you?"

"I was already inside. I only saw her by chance, and she went away before I finished dithering about whether to go back out and approach her."

"Good lord."

"Did she show up at the psychiatric examination?"

"Yes, she did."

"Did she say why she'd been here?"

"She didn't mention being here at all, and I certainly wasn't going to ask. So you went to The Building—"

"What you must understand is that I had the impression that she was getting ready to confide in me. A sort of rapport seemed to be developing. But then John appeared and ushered her out, and it came to nothing."

"It was probably nothing anyway."

"Perhaps so. But I found myself wishing the conversation had developed. And then she turned up outside my building, and once more I failed to seize the chance to hear her out."

"She really got to you."

She knew how to use whom. "So, having to visit The Building anyway, I arranged to get there early, and I went up and knocked on her door."

"You—are you serious?"

"It was presumptuous, I realize. She's your client. In any event, I knocked, and the door popped open. And there she was—" Aware of melodrama, Martha flattened her voice. "There she was, dead on her kitchen floor."

"It *opened?*"

"It seems it doesn't latch unless you slam it."

"And you just walked in?"

"Quite stupid, in hindsight."

"And she was—my God, I was just with her last night."

"Just so."

"She had the psychiatric, and then we stopped at a McDonald's. I had a cup of coffee and she got some takeout." She shook her head. "I can't believe she left the door open."

"I don't think she did," said Martha. "Tessie Doone, my client, said Wilma normally slams the door, because of that problem with the latch, and she heard her slam it last night when she came home.''

''Heard?''

''Tessie lives on the third floor, so all she saw through the peephole in her door was Wilma going upstairs. But she heard her slam the door. Do you know anything about Wilma's relationship with a Mr. Mc-Inerny?''

''Is he involved? Luther would love that.''

''Tessie heard them quarreling outside his apartment door before Wilma came upstairs.''

''Your Tessie's the town crier.''

''She's confined to a wheelchair. I imagine these public dramas are an interesting change from television.''

''Did she by any chance see him go up?''

''Wilma went up alone, Tessie said. Presumably he could have come up later. I suppose Wilma would have let him in.''

''In that building, I'd expect it to be a druggie or something, coming in the fire escape to rip something off.''

''The television was still there. In fact, it was turned on. And she was wearing her nightgown. I suppose that might further implicate McInerny.''

''What about that big leather tote bag she was always carrying around?''

''I didn't see it, but I certainly didn't search the apartment. I'm sure the police will be calling you. I told them you were handling a case for her. They're trying to find out the next of kin.''

''That'd be Geraldine, I guess.''

''Is that the sister?''

"Oh, my God." A bark of laughter. "They've won."

"Just so. One wonders how she will feel about winning like this." Martha put her hands on the arms of her chair to push herself upright. Tension had settled in her knees. "Now one will never know what Wilma wanted to confide."

Enid's telephone beeped. She put her hand on it, but before lifting it she said, "I doubt if there was anything to know, Martha. She was a very odd duck."

THIS TIME JOHN looked up as she came to his door. "Your office is ready," he said. The all-nighter was evident in his face. His skin was milky pale, and dark circles rimmed his eyes.

"I've already moved in," said Martha. "It's splendid. You appear to be still at it."

He grimaced. "I might as well have slept the sleep of the just. At 5:00 a.m., totally sloshed on caffeine, I realized I had picked up the argument by the wrong handle, and I've been performing major surgery all morning. I don't know if I can manage another night. You don't stay eighteen forever."

"Who would want to? John, when you have a chance, we must confer about Tessie Doone's SSI case."

"Oh, right. Your house call." He leaned back. "Let's do it."

She took a chair. "It turns out her name is on a joint bank account."

"Not uncommon."

"I suppose not." She reported Tessie's explanation of the bank account.

"The poor man's will," said John. "Did she request a hearing?"

"No. I'm about to, if you approve."

He smiled. "Take it and run."

"There seems to be no chance of the cousin's making the trip from Philadelphia to testify," she said.

"Not to worry. It's only an administrative hearing. You won't need his body if they can get an affidavit."

"Kareem seemed to think they could."

"And back it up with corroborative stuff. Maybe a statement from the bank to the effect that all activity in the account has been generated by the cousin and not by Tessie. Assuming banks keep that kind of record."

"And assuming," she said, "that it's true." He raised his eyebrows and she said, "I do not entirely believe in this cousin."

"No?"

"I could be quite wrong. But I noticed that it was Kareem who took the lead on answering my questions about the bank account. And then it occurred to me that the putative Kevin Hill and the genuine Kareem Hewitt have the same initials."

"Mm. People do share initials."

"Just so. I also learned from Tessie that Kareem has recently been paroled after serving time for something bargained down from armed robbery."

"You don't say."

"It occurred to me—only as a hypothesis, you understand—that at some time after the crime and before the arrest Kareem might have gone down to Philadelphia, opened an account under a false name with the proceeds from that enterprise, and made his grandmother a joint depositor so that she could send him money in prison, if it so fell out that he had to go to prison. I understand that money is useful in prison.''

"So I've heard.''

"As I said, I could be quite wrong. They could have seemed evasive only because we don't, as it were, speak quite the same language.'' She could no longer evade the sensational. "And then, there was considerable distraction as well.'' Shock was no longer manifesting itself in tremors; once more it was frivolity that assailed her. "On the way to the client,'' she said, "I seem to have happened upon a homicide.''

"Good lord, Martha, it's only your second day.''

"This sort of thing normally happens later?''

"Well, as a rule we like to give people a month or two.''

"The victim, you may be interested to know, is our visitor of yesterday, Wilma Oberfell.''

"Wilma—good lord. I thought you meant something in the street. What happened to her?''

So once more Martha told the story.

"You walked right in?''

"Quite idiotic.''

"Amazing.''

"If you recall,'' said Martha, "yesterday she was announcing that she couldn't trust anybody.''

"So she was. It looks like she was right.''

"I do wonder whom she mistrusted.''

"The question looms, doesn't it? Maybe the world at large?''

"Paranoia?''

"Not at all. The way the world treats our clients, generalized mistrust is the essence of sanity.''

"I wish I'd listened to her. But Howard had just been warning me about the Mother Teresa syndrome.''

"He's talking to himself, you know. If you let clients get to you, you're on burnout road."

"She knew how to use whom."

"Oh, well," he said, "that'll do it."

SEVEN

TILTED BACK in his chair, his fingers laced behind his head, Howard listened without comment but with eloquent changes of expression.

"McInerny," he said. "That's a nuisance. He's treasurer of the tenants association."

Martha said, "I'm inclined to believe there's more to the story than Mr. McInerny."

"Meaning?"

"My impression is that her mistrust centered here in the office."

"Explain."

"Well, she bypassed the receptionist, as if not wanting her presence broadcast. She wanted to see the person in charge and nobody else, she clammed up the moment John appeared, and she said we weren't to tell Enid she had been in. And finally, it was after I told her it was my first day at the office that she began to look like confiding in me."

"Succinct as always." Howard rocked. "That doesn't have to imply that staff was involved. The tenants are all members of the plaintiff class in the rent strike. She might think the staff would cover up for any of them, for the sake of the case." He unlocked his fingers and tilted himself upright. "We'll have to bring Luther in." He swiveled back to his desk, picked up his phone, and punched two digits. "Luther," he said, "would you please come by for a few minutes? Something has come up that may turn into a problem."

Suddenly exhausted, Martha closed her eyes. But the loss of visual clues made her head swim, and she opened them again.

A knock at the door was followed by the rattle of the knob and the entrance of the immensely tall, extremely black man who was Luther Young, director of the Landlord-Tenant Unit. He was wearing a well-cut suit, a white shirt and striped tie, and a scowl.

"Luther," said Howard. "Thank you for giving me some of your valuable time. Martha has some disturbing news for us."

Luther Young nodded to Martha, took a chair, rested his elbows on the arms, and steepled his fingers. During the narrative, he changed neither his posture nor his expression. When it became evident that she had reached the end, he said, "Thank you, Mrs. Patterson."

Martha said, "You're welcome, Mr. Young."

Howard said, "So, Luther."

Luther Young turned his gaze from Martha to Howard and back to Martha. It was the cue for her exit.

She reached to the floor for her handbag and stood up. Her movement brought Luther Young to his feet. With a nod at Howard, she left, closing the door behind her.

She felt unspeakably weary. As she made her way up the corridor toward her office, she looked at her watch and found that it was past two o'clock. Her mind geared up sufficiently to remark that hunger must be contributing substantially to this state of being. She collected her coat and signed herself out for lunch.

She found a bagel shop two doors up. In the steamy heat, she ordered the $5.95 all-day breakfast special: two eggs scrambled in butter and a heavily buttered pumpernickel bagel; she emptied three plastic tubs of half-and-half into her coffee instead of asking for the tin pitcher of 2 percent milk. She partly redeemed the indulgence by conscientiously downing a large orange juice at a seventy-five-cent premium.

Martha's father, the Honorable Justice Jeffreys, had endowed his daughter not only with his acute analytic intelligence and his professional influence but also with the metabolism that had kept him physically spare and mentally alert to the age of ninety-three. He had finally succumbed, not to any failure of the cardiovascular system, but to a speeding car he failed to observe as he jaywalked from his office to the courthouse across the street. Nevertheless, it would not do to abuse one's genetic privileges. This intemperate lunch had served its purpose; she would not repeat it any time soon.

AT FOUR-FORTY, as she sat at her desk with Tessie Doone's file open before her and the phone at her ear, waiting on the Social Security Administration's hold, the elfin paralegal named Anita Pagan appeared at her door carrying a handful of five-by-eight cards.

Martha hung up the phone.

Anita said, "I don't want to interrupt."

"Hold can't be interrupted," said Martha. "It can only be terminated, and I have chosen to do so."

Anita sat down and fanned three cards in front of her. "I just got off intake. John said to try to find you a case that needs to go to court, but all I got were Fair Hearings."

Doing her homework before coming on board at West Brooklyn, Martha had noticed this curious nomenclature. A Fair Hearing was an administrative hearing at which a welfare recipient could appeal from an unfavorable action of the welfare system. Howard had explained that the phrase was a term of art arising from a long-ago Supreme Court decision, not necessarily descriptive of the thing itself. Anita, like all advocates for the needy, made it one word—Fairhearing. "Anyway," she said, "they're typical. John said give you typical if I couldn't give you exciting."

"This early in the game," Martha said, "everything is likely to be exciting."

Anita's lips curved into a surprised little comradely grin. "I still get excited," she said.

The three cases exhibited a variety of tangles in the administration of food stamps and public assistance. "On the face of it," Martha remarked, "these look like agency errors."

"About ninety-nine to one they are," Anita said.

"And such obvious errors are typical?"

"Ask John." The elfin little grin once more. "Except he doesn't think they're errors."

"He suspects malice?"

"Don't get him started. Martha, is it true about you finding Enid's client murdered in The Building?"

Perhaps not quite the speed of light, but near enough.

"GOOD EVENING, Mrs. Patterson," said the doorman. "How are you this evening?" The question seemed to be more than routine; evidently Boris thought she was exhibiting cause for concern.

She had been thinking how good it would be if she could lie back on the chaise, sip from a very hot cup of tea, and spread the whole dismaying business before Edwin's agile mind, and about how it was never again to be.

This would not do. She straightened her shoulders—she hadn't realized they were slumping—and rearranged her lip muscles into what she intended for a smile. "I'm well, thank you, Boris. And you?"

To her surprise, Boris stepped aside from his podium and bowed his head to her level. With the air of whispering in her ear, although his mouth remained a decorous eighteen inches from the side of her head, he murmured, "Someone was inquiring about you."

Obviously someone not meeting Boris's difficult standards of respectability. She said, "Yes?"

"A policeman."

Ah.

"In plain clothes. He was inquiring about your... uh...'movements'"—Boris's voice put quotation marks around the word—"of last night."

Not at all the sort of thing Boris would regard as seemly. "Just so," she stalled. Then, lowering her own voice, she simulated taking him into her confidence. "I had the bad luck to—" How to put this? To discover the probably strangled body of a client? Dear God. "To witness an accident. A fatal accident. I suppose the police want to"—she made it as stuffy as possible—"assess my veracity, in case I'm ever wanted to testify." Given the fullness of her own knowledge, it sounded abominably lame. "I trust you told him the unvarnished truth."

Oh, yes, yes. To the extent that he knew of her "movements" of last evening, Boris had indeed told the unvarnished truth.

There was nothing to interest her in the mail. Up on the seventeenth floor, the apartment seemed overheated. She dropped five fund-raising pleas and three catalogs into the wastebasket, opened three windows, went back to the bedroom and stripped off her professional uniform, showered for a long time under stinging hot water, and then redressed herself in the hot pink velour jumpsuit that Edwin had given her for Christmas more than a dozen years ago.

This terrible weariness, she told herself, was depression. The rule, therefore, was *Move the Body*.

She put on the old Jane Fonda tape and began the workout.

It was no good. She weighed four hundred pounds.

She switched off the tape. *This is not depression, you nitwit; this is grief. One weeps.*

She curled up on the chaise, buried her face in her veloured arms, and forced herself past her ingrained self-possession into the freedom of sobs that lurked just behind that wall. By now, it took only five or six minutes. Then she sat up, blew her nose, and found herself hungry. She picked up the phone and punched in the Chinese takeout down the street.

Wilma Oberfell's death, upstaged by an accusation of police brutality in the South Bronx, did not make the ten o'clock news.

EIGHT

THE *TIMES* had not considered Wilma Oberfell's death to be news that was fit to print; the story did not leap from ambush among the mergers and Chapter 11 reorganizations in the *Wall Street Journal* or shriek from the front pages of *Newsday*, the *News*, or the *Post*. Martha did not need to examine their inner pages; the shockable among her acquaintances did not read *Newsday*, the *News*, or the *Post*.

She was well into her workday, checking her calculation of a client's food stamp allotment and thinking about lunch, when she was startled to see at her door the trim pantsuited figure, coppery complexion, and well-shaped cornrowed head of Detective Vera Jamison. "I just need a few minutes," Detective Jamison said.

"I assume," said Martha, waving her in, "your appearance here means that Wilma Oberfell didn't die of natural causes."

Detective Jamison raised her left arm, crooked it at the elbow, and jerked it toward her chest. It was a disconcertingly violent gesture. "Somebody got her in an armlock. I want you to think back and see if there's anything you didn't think of when we talked yesterday."

Yesterday was a jumble. Martha closed her eyes. The effort produced a memory. "I felt a breeze when the door opened, as if there was a window open somewhere. Might someone have broken in?"

"The fire escape window was open, and it looks like somebody went through her bag. When she was here in the afternoon—any new thoughts on that?"

Martha shook her head.

"Did she mention Francis McInerny?"

"No."

"Do you know if anybody has seen him or talked with him since then?"

"I don't know. Is he missing?"

"Maybe."

"Your best source would be someone in the Landlord-Tenant Unit. Perhaps Luther Young, the unit director—"

"He doesn't know."

The telephone beeped. Martha said, "Excuse me," and picked it up. The clamor of daytime television assaulted her ear. She shouted, *"This is Martha Patterson."*

"Yeah, Miz Patters," said Tessie Doone through the clamor.

"I can hardly hear you," shouted Martha.

"Oh, yeah. Wait a minute, I go turn it down."

Detective Jamison said, "Thank you," and left.

The clamor on the telephone abated to a quiet quacking, and Tessie returned. "I get a letter for a Fair Hearin," she said. One word: *Fairhearing.* "You be my lawyer?"

Martha said, "What is it about?"

"Vibelle's welfare."

Vibelle. The niece. "What's happening with Vibelle's welfare?"

"They cuttin it off. These people ain got enough homeless, now they gon put us on the street."

"What reason do they give?"

"I got it here. They say, 'Vibelle Faraday's unreported income.' Vibelle ain got no unreported income. I tole my worker bout that job long time ago, when Vibelle get her workin papers. She say that ain no problem, Saturdays and Sundays, but then they send me this letter."

"When did you get it?"

"Back roun Halloween. Some witch send it out, I guess. I call up an ax for a Fairhearin, now they givin it to me."

Martha cast her mind back through her homework. "How old is Vibelle?"

"Sixteen."

"And she's in school full-time?"

"She don miss school for nothin. I cain hardly get her to stay home when she sick. She makin honor roll purtnear ever term. They cain jus cut her off like that, it ain right."

Tessie was right. "When is the hearing?"

"Say here December fourteen. You be my lawyer?"

Next Thursday. Perhaps she should check with John. But she was annoyed with *them,* and she said, "Yes. Yes, I will, Ms. Doone." She thought of the OUT OF ODER elevator. "How are you going to get to the hearing?"

"I ain gettin nowhere. I tell em I cain get out none, they havin it here at my apartment. Ten a.m. in the mornin. You gon be here, right?"

"Yes, I will. Now here's what you'll have to do to get ready." She enumerated the documents that would be needed. "I must see them and make copies before the hearing. Could someone stop by the office with them?"

"I guess maybe Kareem. Maybe on the way to work, that be OK?"

Kareem. Oh well. "Yes, that's fine. And while you're on the phone, did Kareem get payment stopped on that money order?"

"Listen, I don know," said Tessie. "Ain nobody know nothin bout that rent gettin stole. Kareem, he go put in the stop, but I don know. Spose that ain so, evbody but me got their rent paid, I got this stop on my money order, what happen? They put us out on the street?"

"Didn't somebody call the other tenants?"

"That's what I'm sayin. *You* tell *me*, but ain nobody else hear nothin. You my lawyer, I do what you say, they cain put us out on the street, can they? They cut off my SSI, an they tryin cut off Vibelle's welfare, an now the police hasslin Kareem bout Wilma gettin kill, we don need no eviction top a all that."

"Tessie, don't worry about being evicted. The rent strike is taking care of that. The police have been questioning Kareem?"

"They go pickin him up after work, takin him down the precinc, axin him all the time where was he Monday night, what do he know bout Wilma—"

"Did they arrest him?"

"Ain got nothin arrest him *for*. They jus hasslin him cause he spen some time upstate. They keep on, they gon make trouble with his parole, an then what we gonna do? That Frank McInerny, he run off somewhere, why ain they out lookin for him steada hasslin Kareem? He livin a straight life now, steady job, be goin to *college* come nex month. They gon mess that up, put us all on the street, they don leave him alone."

And what was one to say? "It must be very unpleasant."

"It be one big mess."

"I'm sure. If he didn't have anything to do with Wilma, I'm sure they'll stop bothering him."

"Miz Patters, he be a black man who done time upstate. They gon take their time fore they leave him alone."

"Well—I'm afraid you're right. At least we should be able to do something about the SSI and the welfare. Have you had a chance to talk to your cousin about the bank account yet?"

"Oh, yeah, Cousin Kevin. Kareem gon talk to him if the police ever get off his case."

"PART-TIME?" asked John.

"Weekends."

"How old?"

"Sixteen."

"In school full-time?"

"Tessie says so."

"Assholes."

Martha smiled. "Tessie is assembling the documentation. I assume we'll win."

Having vented, he relaxed and answered the smile. "No contest. Home hearing, the city will probably default. You could prep her and let her go *pro se*."

"I promised I'd represent her."

"Rookies, I love them. Listen, though, are you sure you want to go back to that place?"

"When one falls off a horse," she said, "it's recommended that one get right back on. But I shan't wander about the building this time."

"I don't suppose you will." He raised his eyes over her head to the doorway. "Carlos, *que pasa?*"

Behind her, she heard, "*Emergencia. Necessito abogado de* welfare." Laboriously, she sorted out, "Emergency. I need a welfare lawyer," as Carlos came on into the office.

The scrape on his temple had scabbed over.

"What's the story?" asked John.

It was evidently another typical one. A mother, three children, no marketable skills, a vanishing husband; denial of a welfare application; mounting rent arrears; a seventy-two-hour notice of eviction; no more stays of eviction available from housing court.

"What's the ground for the EAF denial?"

"Crap," said Carlos. "A fascist worker. She had a Fairhearing this morning, but that's too late."

"Eviction scheduled?"

"Not tomorrow. Could be Friday."

John said to Martha, "They call it an expedited hearing, but it takes two weeks for the decision to come down." She nodded, exercising neck muscles tightened by vicarious anxiety. "OK," he said, "this is where you learn how to do the emergency 78."

She had studied the procedure as part of her homework. She said, "I do?"

A smile. "I know. It's scary the first time, but you'll get used to it. All the forms are in the file. It'll mean walking the papers through Supreme in the morning until a stay of eviction is signed; after that it's cake."

"I think I'm being hazed."

Again the smile. "I'll be here."

"You'd better be."

SITTING TO ONE SIDE of Carlos's desk, Martha realized the meaning of Howard's "highly valued paralegal."

Carlos had obviously done this sort of thing repeatedly. The impertinence he had exhibited in Howard's office was tamed into quiet competence. Martha shared the client's growing relief as questions and answers resolved the chaos of anxiety into the routine of litigable issues.

Twice, Martha saw Vera Jamison walk by in the hall, peer into the office, then pass by.

By a few minutes before five all the papers had been typed, signed, notarized, copied, and collated, and the client, substantially reassured, had departed. Martha sat back and said, "Whew."

Carlos grinned, his teeth flashing white below his bandit mustache. "You get used to it." He pulled open a bottom drawer, pulled out a half-empty packet of Mallomars, and offered them.

Not until then did she realize that she had missed lunch. She took one. "I see you're healing," she said and took a bite. The gooey sweetness was unbelievably restorative.

Carlos touched the scab gently. "Yeah. I got lucky."

She swallowed and said, "Carlos, there's something I have to ask you about."

His, "Mm?" was muffled by his own mouthful of Mallomar.

"I'm handling an SSI case for one of the rent-strike tenants. Tessie Doone."

"The lady in the wheelchair."

"I spoke with her on the phone Monday afternoon, so of course I told her about the theft of the rent money and advised her to stop payment on her money order."

He stuffed the rest of the Mallomar into his mouth and mumbled, "That's good."

"The problem is, I was speaking with her again this afternoon, and she said nobody else in the building seems to know about the theft."

"Hey. That's not good."

"I agree."

His mouth once more clear, he said, "You know what happened? I had this emergency. Soon's I got back from telling Howard, a client came in with a seventy-two-hour notice. Not as bad as today; she just needs a little more time to pay. She couldn't wait; it was getting late in the day. So what I did, I called McInerny. He's the guy that makes the tenants association happen."

"So I've heard."

"I told him what happened, you know, to the money, and I told him to go around the building and tell people they better stop payment. See, I figured he's right on the spot, he can do it faster than me making forty-some-odd phone calls, which I didn't have time for if this lady wasn't going to get evicted. And they don't all of them have telephones anyway."

"I see," said Martha.

"Sounds like he didn't do it."

"Have you heard that he's missing?"

"McInerny?"

"Hasn't Detective Jamison talked with you?"

"Detective?"

"A woman with cornrows. She's investigating Wilma Oberfell's death."

"No kidding. I was over at a Housing Authority hearing all day, and this client was waiting when I got back. He's missing? Sheesh." He touched the scab absently. "Listen; you want to know something?"

"About Mr. McInerny?"

"It sounds crazy, but—listen, what if it was him planned that mugging?"

"Good heavens."

"See, what was funny was how those dudes zeroed right in on me. They were hanging out in the street, right? I went down the station, they came down the station right behind me. I go through the gate, they come through the gate, they muscle in around me, I feel this thing poking me." He jabbed his right thumb against his ribs. "They tell me it's a knife. And what happens, the first thing they go for is that portfolio. Like they know it's got money. They grab that, and then, like it's an afterthought, you know, they dig in my pocket for my wallet. And then they split."

Martha said, "Interesting."

"So, you know, if they know there's money in there, how do they know? Somebody's gotta tell them, right?"

"And you think that was Mr. McInerny?"

"Hey, he's the one who put it there. What else I was thinking, if they know there's money, they know most of it's checks and money orders, right? And you don't just waltz into a check-cashing place with a box of checks and money orders made out to somebody else and walk out with the money. You gotta have some kind of organization."

Martha said, "Are you suggesting that Mr. McInerny might be associated with an organization with the resources to cash checks made out to Brooklyn Housing Court?"

"Well, look at all the money laundering goes on. McInerny's Irish, right?"

"His name would indicate that."

"So what I'm thinking, what if he's hooked up with

that outfit that's always blowing things up in London? The IRS?''

"IRA," said Martha. "Irish Republican Army."

"Whatever. You tell me he didn't pass on the word to the tenants to stop payment. Sounds to me like he was giving somebody time to get those checks and money orders cashed."

"Perhaps he just didn't follow through. I've heard that he's an alcoholic. He simply might not be particularly trustworthy."

"Whatever." Carlos fingered his mustache. "Did you tell Howard?"

"No." She saw a fractional relaxation of tension. "But he needs to know."

"You gonna tell him?"

"That's your responsibility."

"Yeah," he said quickly. He pulled open a file drawer next to his desk. "First, I better make those calls myself. Maybe it isn't too late, they can still get payment stopped. I just as soon have some good news, you know, before I go talk to Howard."

NINE

WALKING the emergency lawsuit through clerks' offices and judges' chambers took up all of the next morning, but at last Martha found a judge with a free moment to sign the stay of eviction and calendar the case for the following Monday.

Most of the unit members had already gone to lunch. Only Anita was there, just taking her brown bag from the refrigerator in the office manager's office. In high spirits, Martha offered to treat her to a celebratory lunch. On their way out, they found Enid Morgan leaning over the receptionist's desk to sign for some papers that had just been served. They invited her to the party; Enid said, "Why not?" and they dodged through lunch-hour foot traffic to a Greek half-storefront on Montague Street.

"I just got served with an order to show cause," Enid said when they had found a table. "They're moving to dismiss Wilma's custody petition."

"Surely there's no urgency," said Martha.

"Well, the case was on the calendar anyway. We were going to adjourn because the psychiatric report wasn't ready, but I guess they thought it'd be a good time to get it over with. I think I'll just stipulate. I don't need to spend half the day in family court just to tell the judge that my client, being dead, doesn't want the kid anymore."

An impulse, born of curiosity and nourished by her meager caseload, nudged Martha. "When is it on?"

"Tomorrow morning."

"Would you be willing to have me appear on the motion?"

Enid's eyebrows went up. "Why?"

"A last service to Wilma Oberfell, I suppose."

"Good grief."

"I found her in a singularly undignified condition, you know. I suppose I feel her case, at least, should be laid to rest with a bit more formality than just a stipulation between attorneys."

Enid shrugged. "If you've got the time, I've got the file."

Anita said, "Who is it has the baby?"

"Three-year-old, actually," said Enid. "Geraldine and Neil Zable. The late Wilma's sister and brother-in-law, who have now prevailed without benefit of adjudication."

Anita said, "I wouldn't think they had anything to worry about, anyway."

"Now they don't."

"I mean not ever."

Enid said, "A nonparent doesn't win unless the birth mother is unfit."

"I saw Wilma around the office. You'd call her fit?"

"Sure, I called her fit. I was her lawyer."

"But would a judge send a little kid to live with her? In The Building? Where do they live?"

"Bay Ridge. In a house with a yard and a swing set. I know what you're thinking, but you're wrong." Enid looked at Martha. "We've got Judge Wallerstein."

"Ah, well," said Martha. She was acquainted with Harry Wallerstein.

"What about Judge Wallerstein?" said Anita.

"He believes," said Enid, "that the act of giving

birth automatically renders a woman fit to rear the child.''

"And if there's an insurmountable problem with the mother," Martha added, "such as her untimely demise, the act of impregnating her goes a long way toward fitting a man for the task."

"No chance there," Enid said. "He died six months ago."

"Was there an estate?"

"Nothing to get excited about. Three or four thousand. It was still in probate the last I heard."

"I could get excited about three or four thousand," Anita said, "but to raise a three-year-old—I guess it wouldn't be much of a motive."

"Motive?" Enid's eyebrows went up again. "You think the Zables offed my client to collect the kid's inheritance?"

That having been the notion that prompted Martha's question, she suppressed a smile.

Anita said, "*Somebody* killed her."

Enid said, "Some druggie broke in looking for loot, and she made the mistake of waking up."

"You're no fun. But I guess you wouldn't want the baby growing up with a murderer." Anita looked at Martha. "John says you're going back to The Building to do a home hearing."

Martha said, "This time I won't go knocking on strange doors."

"Do you know any self-defense stuff?"

"Karate? That sort of thing?"

"Sort of. The union got a self-defense course at management expense in the last contract."

"On-the-job risks are that serious?"

"Well, nobody's ever attacked me, but the union

thought it was important. I guess the contract wouldn't cover you, but I think they gave management a special rate. I know Howard went, and—'' She stumbled. ''And some other management people.''

Anita had avoided naming someone. John, perhaps? Something interesting there.

''Save your money,'' said Enid.

Anita said, ''It's a good course. You took it.''

''I took it, and it's bull.''

''The idea,'' said Anita, ''is to let the guy know you're not an easy mark. They'd rather pick on somebody who doesn't know how to fight.''

''That's the party line. What about guys who get turned on by a fight? Don't fool around. Get a gun.''

''A *gun!*'' Anita laid down her falafel-in-pita and placed both hands flat on the table on either side of her plate. She looked like an angry kitten about to spring. ''Enid, do you know how many innocent people get killed by guns?''

''Amateurs. Learn how to use it. If Wilma Oberfell had had a gun by her bed Monday night, Martha wouldn't be answering a motion to dismiss tomorrow morning. Listen; if women would get comfortable with guns, half my caseload would be unnecessary.''

''Or in jail.'' Anita picked up her stuffed pita. ''Or dead.''

Enid smiled and attacked her shish kebab. Martha continued quietly demolishing her stuffed grape leaves.

Presently Anita looked at Martha and said, ''I hope you're coming to the Christmas party.''

The invitation had been in her mailbox that morning. Expressing reservations would be surly: Anita was on the party committee, as was John. Martha said, ''I will if I can.''

LEAVING THE RESTAURANT, she saw a mustached figure going in the door of an OTB office across the street. "Isn't that Carlos?" she said.

"I didn't see," said Anita.

TAKING A KEY RING from her handbag and unlocking a file drawer, Enid said, "I'll bet that detective doesn't do undercover work. One look and you'd know her forever. I thought cornrows went out twenty years ago."

Martha had gone to her office for the Wilma Oberfell file. "Detective Jamison spoke with you, I take it," she said.

"For all the good it did her. She was hot on the trail of that trust thing, on which I'm a total blank."

"Trust—" For a moment Martha's mind veered off into her former field of practice. "Oh. You mean Wilma's looking for somebody to trust."

"Not while I was with her, and I told Detective Cornrows that in seven positions. Then we had a session about McDonald's."

"Something happened at McDonald's?"

"It's what didn't happen at McDonald's. Meaning, Wilma didn't eat anything there; she got takeout. She said she still had a nervous stomach from the psychiatric, but she'd be fine by the time she got home. Detective Cornrows said she died a couple of hours after she ate the stuff."

"She did eat it, then."

"They found the wrappers in her garbage and the remains in her digestive tract." She pulled out a folder and handed it to Martha. "Your prayer book for the last rites." The keys jingled as she pushed the drawer closed.

"You lock your files?" said Martha.

"Just this one." Enid pulled the drawer open again, reached behind the folders, and lifted out a miniature television. "I have to protect my toy."

"Nice. When do you have time to watch?"

Enid laughed and tucked it back behind the folders. "Only after hours since Howard took over."

HER CASELOAD being less than burdensome, Martha took the time to read all of Wilma's file.

The child's name was Rosemary. Rosemary Oberfell; Wilma had not, after all, been married to the child's father. Anthony Collins had died just over six months ago, on May 23.

The papers submitted by Geraldine and Neil Zable presented them as responsible citizens with two children, aged fifteen and twenty. Neil Zable affirmed himself to be the owner of A-Z Appliances, a string of appliance and electronics stores located in Brooklyn, Queens, and Long Island. With Wilma's consent, Rosemary had been placed in foster care with the Zables a few days after her birth. Geraldine had transferred her work of keeping the firm's accounts to a home computer. They asserted that the child had formed a bond with them, the breaking of which would do incalculable harm to her emotional health and well-being.

Martha turned back to the first court document, Wilma's original petition to regain custody. It was dated June 24.

So Rosemary had lived with Geraldine and Neil Zable for two and a half years with no action on Wilma's part to recover the child. Then, only a month after Anthony Collins's death, Wilma had commenced this proceeding—a proceeding that the Zables had vigorously opposed.

Did the timing mean anything? Enid said the father had left an estate of only three or four thousand dollars, but for forty years Martha had been devising ways to pass along assets without their appearing in a probate file.

She was growing curious about Geraldine and Neil Zable.

TEN

MARTHA TOLD HERSELF she really must attend the Christmas party. She would not willingly slight either Anita or John. And then, she had drawn a name in the gift exchange—a secretary in Family Law, she had learned by consulting her staff roster—and someone else had drawn hers. She would have to drop into a thing shop to pick up a gift. Probably a coffee mug.

She was strolling toward the subway with no demands on her evening when she recalled seeing a branch library a few blocks farther up Court Street. She went on and found it still open. She filled out an application for a Brooklyn Public Library card and went into the reading room.

The catalog listed books on unarmed self-defense. Two of them were on the shelf. She took one down. It seemed, actually, quite sensible, and it would make a change from the rereading of *Pride and Prejudice* upon which she had embarked. She used her new card, descended into the subway, and arrived at her walled and sentried castle.

Boris nodded toward the settee in the ficus grove. "Someone to see you, Mrs. Patterson."

She turned. A man got to his feet and said, "Ms. Patterson?" He was of medium height; his skin was medium brown; his conservatively barbered hair was of African texture. He was dressed unremarkably in gray flannel slacks and a leather aviator jacket and moved like someone who carried responsibility without anxiety. Perhaps he was a plainclothes policeman.

"I don't think we've met," she said.

"No, we haven't. My name's Harris. You're Martha Patterson?"

"Yes, I am. What can I do for you, Mr. Harris?"

"I was asked to look you up"—he smiled slightly—"by somebody else you haven't met."

"Oh?" Perhaps reality was on the point of outclassing Jane Austen.

Harris said, "I'm a friend of Francis McInerny."

MARTHA SAID, "I took you for a police officer." She had removed their conversation to a Sixth Avenue coffee shop, several blocks out of reach of Boris's curiosity.

Harris tore open a packet of sugar and emptied it into his coffee, crumpled the packet into a tiny ball, and put it in the saucer. "Just a friend of Frank's."

"I've never met Mr. McInerny, you know."

"I know. He says he knows of you through a friend of his. A lady named Wilma Oberfell."

"Does he know Wilma Oberfell is dead?"

"He said to tell you he didn't kill her."

"I see. Where is he?"

"Well, I'm not really at liberty to tell you that. Not right now."

"Why is he hiding?"

"He's scared."

"If he wasn't responsible for Wilma's death, I should think he'd have less to fear by coming forward than by hiding." Harris's gesture could best be described, she supposed, as a courteous shrug. She took a sip of her coffee and allowed herself a readjustment of attitude. "What is it he wants from me?"

"I'm not sure. He's not in the greatest state of mind. The best I can say is, he wants to know—"

The waiter slapped a plate in front of Martha. "BLT on whole-wheat toast. Change your mind, sir? Something to eat? More coffee?"

"Nothing, thanks," said Harris. The waiter departed and Harris said, "I guess you could say he wants to know where you fit in."

Martha had ordered the sandwich purely in order to secure them a booth at early dinner hour. She let it lie on the plate. "I'm an attorney, semiretired, and this week I started a spell of pro bono work at West Brooklyn Legal Services."

"That would explain why Frank didn't know you from before."

"Just so." She sipped coffee. "Mr. Harris, I have nothing but your word that you're acting on his behalf."

"That's true."

"You could be a reporter. Or a policeman. If that's what you are, this conversation is pointless, since I've already told the police everything I know about Wilma Oberfell. Or, of course, you might be someone who wishes him ill on your own account."

Harris appeared unperturbed. "That's true; I could be. I'm not."

"I'm inclined to believe you, but I'm aware that I have an unduly trusting nature. I will speak with Mr. McInerny directly, if he wishes, but not through a go-between."

"Fair enough," said Harris.

"And you can tell him this. My relationship to West

Brooklyn Legal Services and its relationship to Mr. McInerny as a member of the tenants association makes Mr. McInerny my client, although in a somewhat tenuous fashion. I understand that he is a onetime member of the bar.''

"A lawyer? He says so, yes.''

"Then he is aware that the Code of Professional Responsibility is heavily weighted on the client's side. Which means that he can trust me to keep his communications confidential.''

"He'll be glad to hear that.'' He slid out of the booth, rummaged in his pocket, laid coins on the table. "I'll tell him what you've said. Thank you for listening, Mrs. Patterson.''

"You're welcome.''

Harris zipped his jacket and made his way to the door.

THE REASONABLE thing to do, of course, would be to eat her sandwich and go home. If Francis McInerny chose to surface, so be it; if not, it was, after all, none of her affair.

But what was at home? Boris's canned greeting, the workout tape, *Pride and Prejudice*.

The coins Harris had left covered the price of his coffee plus a precise 15 percent tip. Martha added enough to bring the total up to both tips; then, leaving the sandwich untouched, she clambered out of the booth and headed for the cashier.

Streetlights and storefronts illuminated the Sixth Avenue sidewalk. When she pushed her way out the door Harris was still in view less than half a block away, heading downtown among the pedestrian traffic.

There was no longer anything much besides her

sense of dignity to prevent Martha from acting as crazily as she wished, and her sense of dignity had begun to bore her. She turned downtown, trailing Harris through the well-lighted December evening.

It turned out to be easier than she expected. Martha had always been a walker. After her aging knees had put an end to tennis, walking remained. She easily maintained a distance of half a block between them. She was helped by the fact that Harris had no inkling that Martha Patterson, that dignified elderly female attorney, was trailing him along the streets of Greenwich Village. If he had looked around with any attention, he would have seen her, but he did not look around. He simply kept walking, and Martha kept walking behind him. She had no qualms. The Village had been her village throughout her New York City lifetime. There was no outdoor place in the city where she felt more secure.

At Fourth Street, Harris turned east. The foot traffic thinned out, and she let the distance between them lengthen. They traversed the southern edge of Washington Square Park past various chunks of New York University, moving with purpose among sauntering students and weaving skaters. Once more the foot traffic thickened. Harris caught the light at Broadway. It turned red just as Martha reached it, and she lost sight of him among the knotted crowd. But she crossed in a hurry when it changed and saw him once more as he waited for the traffic to clear at Lafayette. He was apparently heading into the East Village, that fluid amalgam of Yuppie-dom and drug-riddled homelessness.

Martha hung a hundred feet back from the intersection until the light changed and Harris crossed; then she hurried forward and plunged across herself. And so they continued, follow the leader and dodge the traffic, until as she was crossing First Avenue, she saw Harris turn aside in the middle of the block ahead and vanish.

When Martha reached the corner, she found a brick wall plastered with flaking strata of posters. Three men dressed in grimy layers leaned against the wall, two of them standing, engaged in a desultory argument, one seated and staring at something outside Martha's range of vision. A fourth lay motionless, a heap of rags, on a grating.

Halfway along the block, a bulb inside a metal cage illuminated four crumbling concrete steps leading down to a littered areaway. At the foot of the steps, a steel door was set flush in the wall. A graffiti-scribbled sign at eye-level said:

ST. HONORIA'S SHELTER

Well.

Surely it was now time to go home. Having tracked Harris to his destination, one could now try looking this place up in the phone book; one could make a call, find out just what St. Honoria's Shelter might be, possibly inquire whether a man named Francis McInerny might be sheltering there.

And then what? *Pride and Prejudice?*

She descended the steps, located a bell push in the frame, and pressed it. Through the heavy door she heard a buzz.

After a few seconds the knob rattled, the door swung inward, and she found herself facing a tall, stooped white man. He was bald from forehead to midcrown, his clean, freckled scalp surrounded by a fringe of long pewter gray hair that one would have expected to be lank, but that was, in fact, fluffy with cleanliness. His thrift-shop clothes were intensely clean, and his long, deeply lined face looked freshly shaved.

A cooking odor drifted out the door—something like vegetable soup. From the far end of the narrow hall that stretched in front of her she heard men's voices.

"Good evening," she said. "My name is Martha Patterson. I'm Mr. McInerny's lawyer. I understand he wants to see me."

"Mr. McInerny?" The doorkeeper's husky voice articulated the six syllables with careful clarity.

"Francis McInerny," said Martha. "I understood that he'd be here. I hope I have the right address."

The doorkeeper hesitated a moment longer, then stepped back. "You want to talk to Father Keenan."

And very likely she did. "Thank you," she said, and stepped through the door. The hall opened at the far end into a large bright space—something, perhaps, on the order of a gymnasium. It was there that the voices and the fragrance of soup originated. She heard male laughter.

The doorkeeper closed the door behind her. She rummaged in her handbag for her card case as he led her up the hall. Halfway along he turned into an open door that gave on a lighted office. A heavyset middle-aged man in a worn black suit and clerical collar sitting at a desk facing the door looked up from a pile of spreadsheets.

"Father," said the doorkeeper, "this lady says she's Frank's lawyer."

"Martha Patterson, Father." She had located her card case; she extracted a generic West Brooklyn card on which, not yet having been issued cards of her own, she had written her name in black ink.

"Good evening, ma'am." Father Keenan pushed back his chair and came around the end of his desk. He walked with a slight limp. He looked at the doorkeeper and said, "Thanks, Bill."

The doorkeeper nodded and backed out the door.

Father Keenan took the card and examined it. "West Brooklyn Legal Services. A man named Young, am I right? Luther Young. Does housing court work."

"You know him."

"I have friends in Catholic Charities for the Diocese of Brooklyn. You keep good company, Ms. Patterson." He waved at a chair and, when she had seated herself, hoisted his rump onto a corner of the desk. "What's the story?"

"Is Francis McInerny here?" she asked.

Father Keenan said, "Now, what would have you thinking that?"

"I don't want anybody to get into trouble because of anything I might say."

He smiled. "What kind of assurance do you want?"

"I suppose...not to come down too hard on anybody who might have behaved imprudently. He hasn't caused any harm."

Father Keenan laughed. "By many people's lights, all of us here are behaving imprudently all the time. And I don't make an exception for you, you know."

"I believe I must thank you for a compliment," she said. "This evening, a young man who said his name was Harris introduced himself to me as a friend of Francis McInerny's."

"Harris, was it?"

"I assume you know that Mr. McInerny has not been

seen in his usual places for the past three days. Mr. Harris and I are both aware that he may be in trouble. Consequently, we were both being cagy and our conversation was inconclusive. But my interest was aroused, so when he left, I followed him.''

"Dear me. That will embarrass him to no end. And now you think we're harboring Frank McInerny.''

"I think he may be here.''

"What do you want with him?''

"Actually, Mr. Harris left me with the impression that it's he who wants to see me. I should explain that by virtue of my work at West Brooklyn, I'm Mr. McInerny's lawyer and bound to keep his confidences.''

"I see. You're still being pretty cagy.''

"Yes, I suppose so. And you as well.''

Father Keenan pushed up his sleeve and consulted a watch. "Would you mind waiting here for a few minutes? Maybe we can arrange to open up what's on all our minds.''

SEVERAL TIMES Martha heard the door buzzer, felt a draft, and saw ragged men—the city's untouchables—pass the open door of Father Keenan's office. At one point she got up from her chair to read a framed text on the wall behind the desk:

> INASMUCH AS YE HAVE DONE IT UNTO ONE
> OF THE LEAST OF THESE, MY BRETHREN,
> YE HAVE DONE IT UNTO ME.

It was Harris who ended her wait, entering the office with his unhurried, purposeful stride. "Well,'' he said. "It really is Mrs. Patterson. And I led you straight here.

It never occurred to me that you might be a reporter or a cop.''

"Surely appearances are against it.''

"All the same, I should have known better.''

"No harm done. Your judgment was accurate. I'm not a reporter or a cop; I'm a pro bono lawyer with Legal Services, just as I said.''

He nodded. "Frank will be along in a minute. Father thought you'd do best in the conference room.''

"I've told you who I am,'' said Martha, following him across the hall to a room with a table and chairs. "Who are you?''

"I'm Harris.'' He flipped the light switch and fluorescence flickered on. "Harris Gordon. I'm a paramedic, training as an alcoholism and drug counselor.''

"And you work here.''

"Part-time.'' He turned the quiet smile on her. "Pro bono.''

ELEVEN

FRANCES X. MCINERNY was a stocky man with a luxury of white hair and bloodshot blue eyes under bushy eyebrows. His square face, which Martha would have expected to be ruddy and jocund, was pale, laced with broken capillaries on cheeks and nose and anxiety lines around the mouth. His navy blue suit was shapeless and shiny at the elbows; his white shirt was clean but unironed; the knot of his frayed tie sagged below a missing collar button. Having introduced them, Harris left, closing the door behind him.

McInerny's, "How d'ye do, Mrs. Patterson," exhibited a trace of brogue. He shook her offered hand and sat down across from her. "I thought to see you under a bit more civilized circumstances, you know, but... here we are."

"Just so," said Martha. "How did you know my address, Mr. McInerny?"

"Ah. She told me. My late good friend Wilma Oberfell, rest her soul." He surprised Martha by executing a discreet sign of the cross. "And what I'm wondering is, how did it come about that you were acquainted with the poor lady?"

"She didn't tell you?"

"No, she did not. She enjoyed being—shall we say—a bit cryptic in her disclosures."

Martha said, "Monday afternoon, Wilma Oberfell appeared at West Brooklyn Legal Services asking to see the person in charge. That's how she phrased it."

"Howard Wallace, that would be."

"Just so. Mr. Wallace wasn't in, and I happened to be in his office. At first, she wouldn't consent to talk with anyone but him, but eventually she seemed about to confide in me. However, we were interrupted, and nothing came of it. Later, she apparently followed me home. I saw her in front of my building, but she went away before I had a chance to accost her."

"Ah."

"Sometime during that night," said Martha, "somebody strangled her."

McInerny ran his hand over his face. "Rest her soul."

Martha said, "Why did you send Harris to scout me?"

"Ah. A fair question, to be sure."

Martha said nothing.

McInerny said, "Harris tells me you see yourself in an attorney-client relationship with myself."

"I must tell you, however, that I have no expertise in criminal law. If you're involved with Wilma Oberfell's death, I must advise you to consult a criminal defense lawyer."

"Well, now," he said, " 'involved' wouldn't be quite the way I'd put it."

"What is it you want from me?"

"Not a criminal defense," he said. "I did nothing to cause the poor lady's death, and if it should come to needing to prove it, I'll go elsewhere. Let's say that what I most need just now is information and a critical ear."

"Very well," said Martha.

FRANCIS MCINERNY'S story began on the Monday. He had collected the rent money and had then gone out, leaving it with Wilma Oberfell to deliver to the West Brooklyn messenger. "The Puerto Rican fellow, Quinones."

Martha nodded.

"And so she did. She was off on her own affairs by the time I returned, but I found the receipt on my table."

At around nine-thirty or ten, he said, Wilma had rung his doorbell. She had wanted to come in, but he had been tired; he had told her as much, and she had gone off up to her own apartment. "I saw her start up the stairs," he said, "and I let her go off without any escort or protection, and it's not an action I take pride in."

"What happened after she went upstairs?"

"Ah, well. A number of things, and some of them I'm not proud to admit to. Yes. Well, the first thing of any importance is, I saw somebody on the fire escape. The place does have fire escapes. The landlord can't undo that, though I'm thinking he wouldn't hurry to turn a hand if they fell off."

He paused. Martha waited.

"But be that as it may. We're both in the F line, Wilma and I, the line of studios, so we share the same fire escape. Now, my place normally has a window blind over that window. I've always kept it pulled down for privacy, but the springs get old on those roller blinds, and the other day it fell apart beyond my fixing. Our landlord'll fix nothing, be it a bathroom or a stair rail or an elevator, without a court order and very likely a motion to find him in contempt as well, so you can guess what kind of attention an old window blind would get." Another pause. "I wasn't used to having that window uncovered. Anything moving outside that window would catch my eye, if you take my meaning.''

''Something caught your eye?''

''A young fellow coming down the fire escape like the hounds of hell were after him.''

''Did you see his face?''

''Not to any purpose. He was wearing a hood pulled down to his eyes.''

''You said he was young?''

''Ah. It was the way he moved, with a spring in his step like a young gazelle.''

''It was after dark, of course.''

''Quite true. But that window faces an alleyway and there's a floodlight on the building opposite. I don't get the full glare, but I'm in what you might call the penumbra. I saw him all right.''

''Does the fire escape go all the way to the ground?''

''Not exactly. It leaves off outside the first-floor window, and at the end there's a ladder hooked to the rail. In a fire you're supposed to unhook it and lower it, though if flames were pouring out the windows God knows how you'd find the time. I suppose this one did what all the agile young ones do: swung himself over the rail, dangled by his hands, and dropped to the alleyway. It's only a matter of ten or twelve feet.''

''Did you see him do that?''

''I did not. He was below my eye-level, and to tell you the truth, I'm cautious about what I let myself observe. There's dealing going on in neighboring buildings, and I didn't know but this was one of them, who'd come across the roofs to escape from the law or from a competing entrepreneur, it might be.''

''What time was this?''

"A bit after Wilma, rest her soul, went upstairs. Fifteen or twenty minutes, maybe."

"Then what happened?"

"Ah, well." McInerny rubbed his face. "To be sure, I'm not proud of the rest of it."

"That's not important," said Martha.

"To be sure. Not important. It's just that, you know, having meant to do no such thing, I had me a drink."

"I see."

"A drink, and another, and so it goes. And as would happen after enough of that, I got to thinking about Wilma again." He sighed. "You'll be needing to know the whole story. It wasn't just talking we were doing at my door. It was a quarrel we were having, and me saying some very unkind things to the poor lady. And as it would do, the time came that I thought I should go up and tell her I was sorry." A pause. "Long ago she gave me the keys to her apartment, and she took mine, in case anything should happen to one of us." Another pause. "So up I went."

"What time was that?"

"I couldn't tell you to the minute," he said, "or even the hour. The building had quieted down a good deal." He rubbed his face again. "I took Wilma's keys in my hand and went up the stairs and unlocked her door."

"It was locked?"

"Indeed it was. A lock and a deadbolt, both of them locked tight. It was dark inside except for the television flickering. I could hear it muttering away, but not another sound. I thought she was likely lying awake, still put out about our quarrel. I said, quiet, you know, 'Wilma?' and there wasn't any answer." His voice faltered, then began again. "I found the light switch and turned it on, thinking to make her admit she was awake. And there she was, lying on the floor in her nightie, with her face...her tongue—''

He broke off and buried his face in both hands.

If Martha had not seen that same sight, she would have found the gesture unendurably melodramatic. ''What did you do?''

''Ah, now.'' A silence. ''That's just what I don't know.''

She stared.

''The next thing I remember, it was daylight and something was thumping on the soles of my shoes.''

''Thumping...?''

''Thumping the soles of my shoes, and I was just coming to. For it isn't sleeping and waking you do, you know. It's passing out and coming to. There I was, lying on hard, cold boards and looking up at two great blue-coated policemen, the near one thumping away at the soles of my shoes with his nightstick.''

''Good heavens.''

''I sat myself up and found myself on somebody's front porch, the police rousting me as if I were some homeless bum passed out against the wall in Grand Central. But it wasn't Grand Central I was in, nor was it Brooklyn, where I was the last time I remembered anything. I had to ask them where I was.''

A pause.

''Where were you?''

Again he rubbed his face. ''White Plains. Respectable suburban White Plains. There I was, sitting myself up from a drunken stupor to answer to a pair of respectable suburban cops and finding myself on the very front porch of my very own home, as used to be before I drank my life away.''

"That must have been disconcerting."

"To say the least. The only blessing in it, it wasn't my ex coming out to pick up the morning *Times* and stumbling over some drunken bum who happened to be myself. Moved out years ago, she did." He sighed. "Being asked for identification, I turned out my wallet and my pockets for them, and for myself as well, for I had no idea what might have become of my personal fortune during those lost hours. What I found was three dollars and seventy-eight cents. Three wrinkled-up singles in my wallet and three quarters and three pennies in my change pocket." He attempted a smile. "You'd think three threes should be lucky."

"Was that less than you'd started with?"

"Indeed, it was. The Social Security was credited on the Saturday. I must have bought myself a ticket to White Plains during those lost hours, and a cab ride from the station, imagining I was back in the old days."

"I see."

"The householder wanted no more than to get me out of his neighbors' sight, so the officers took me down to the station and bought me a ticket to the city, and there I was, riding the eight-oh-one to Grand Central, just like the old days."

Martha said, "That was Tuesday morning."

"And this is Thursday evening. And what have I been doing since? Well, my dear lady, when Metro-North landed me back in Grand Central, I bethought me of this blessed place. I stayed here once years ago, at another bad time."

"A homeless shelter."

"A haven."

"Of course," said Martha, "you aren't homeless."

"And it's not much longer their charity will put up with my affluent presence. But think about it. The last thing in my memory, before waking to the merry tattoo of a nightstick on my shoe soles, was the sight of my dear friend Wilma, lying on her kitchen floor in her nightie, with her face like a Halloween mask."

"Just so."

"You'll never have suffered alcoholic hallucinations. Pink elephants, we called it when I was a kid, and laughed ourselves silly. I'm finding the humor has worn thin. There I was, riding into the city, almost the respectable Westchester commuter, and in my mind the horror of that scene. And you see...I didn't know if I'd seen it or hallucinated it."

"I see."

"Either way, you know, it was a horror. It might be the straitjacket was just around the corner. Or it might be I wasn't quite to the pink elephants yet and it was a real scene I was seeing—my old friend Wilma, dead on the floor, looking like something out of a horror movie."

"Yes."

"And if it was real, then there'd be New York's finest asking, 'Where were you on the night of?' and such. And, you see, I didn't *know*."

"Yes, I see."

"This was the only place for me."

"I see."

"Hi," said Francis McInerny. "My name's Frank, and I'm an alcoholic."

THE WHITE PLAINS part of this yarn could be verified, of course, and McInerny hadn't been hallucinating the scene in Wilma's apartment. The question, of course, was whether he had created it. That alcoholic blackout was very convenient.

"Please," said Martha, "tell me when it was that Wilma told you my name and address."

"Ah." He rubbed his face. "She'd left a slip of paper in my apartment. Your name and where it is you live."

"Why do you suppose she did that?"

"Making a note for herself, I should imagine, and then going off and forgetting to take it with her. I must have picked it up and tucked it into a pocket, thinking to return it to her. For in a pocket is where I found it when I got here."

Not impossible, Martha supposed.

"And then, finding myself in the position I'm in— well, I thought I should find out who you might be, you know."

"Do you have it with you now?"

"I'm sorry to say I do not. This is a blessed place, but a place to keep your files in order it is not."

"Perhaps Harris has it."

McInerny shook his head. "I read it off to him and he made a note of his own. Yesterday, that would have been; and then in the hurly-burly of the day it went off about its own affairs, as slips of paper have a way of doing."

It was not altogether satisfactory, but further questions seemed unlikely to produce anything better just then. Martha said, "When Wilma came to the office that Monday afternoon, she said she was looking for somebody to trust. Do you know what she might have meant?"

"I do not. Though it sounds like her. She was uncommonly fond of indirection. *Imply* a lot of meaning, as if the two of you shared a secret. Allude to things better left unspoken, like parents talking in front of the children, if you take my meaning.''

Martha had an acquaintance with just such a habit of speech.

''It took a good deal of question and answer to get her to spit out just what it was she might be alluding *to*. And then you might find, so to speak, that there was a good deal of *ill*usion in the *all*usion.''

Martha allowed herself a smile. ''I take it, then, you don't know what she might have been mistrustful of.''

''You take it correctly.''

After a moment's consideration, Martha said, ''Were you aware that the rent money was stolen?''

''Stolen! Holy saints, how did that happen?''

''Carlos Quinones says three men threatened him with knives in the subway and took the portfolio containing the rent.''

''Holy saints.''

''I understand a good many of the payments were in the form of money orders.''

''For the most part. Three or four of the tenants run to checking accounts, and there are two who always pay in cash, not wanting to put out the fee for a money order.''

''Carlos said he phoned you late in the afternoon and asked you to go around and tell people to stop payment on the checks and money orders.''

''Said that, did he? Well, that he did not do.''

''Do you have an answering machine?''

''An old thing from better days, but it still works, and there was no message that day, for it was turned on when I came in and the light was not blinking. I remember looking, for I was hoping for a message that never came.''

''Perhaps Carlos left a message with Wilma and she forgot to tell you.''

''That I would doubt. She would have left me a note. She delighted in leaving notes.''

There was a short silence.

''Tell me,'' said Martha, ''did Wilma have a habit of following people around?''

''Ah. She had some strange ways, poor lady.''

''She did follow people?''

''She could make herself hard to notice. She'd be one car back on the subway, or she'd walk on the other side of the street, that sort of thing. She couldn't manage anybody in a car, of course; a lady on a fixed income can't be jumping into a taxi and crying out, 'Follow that car!' But not many in her acquaintance drive cars. It was a compulsion, you might say, something to be ashamed of, not brought into the light of day.''

''How did you know about it, then?''

''Ah, well. Things would come up in our conversations that I didn't think she could know without being, so to speak, on my trail. I took to watching for her and observed her at it a time or two. So I waited for her one time and spoke to her as if our meeting was just a pleasant chance. And later she confessed. That's how she thought of it, you see—not as a thing of fun, fit for conversation and joking, but a thing of shame, to be confessed.'' He folded his hands on the table. ''I'm wondering if we have the same thing in mind.''

Highly valued paralegal.

''Short and skinny, like all those Puerto Rican men,'' said McInerny. ''And young and active—''

Carlos. Martha found herself wishing she had not set this train of thought rolling down the track. She said, "How long was it after Wilma went up that you saw this figure on the fire escape?"

"Not long. Half an hour or less."

"Did you have the television or radio on?"

"There's no luck there. My TV's on the blink, and I don't bother much with the radio. What they call music these days isn't to my taste, and without a car, the traffic reports aren't of much interest. But it wasn't long. Twenty minutes, most likely; hardly half an hour."

"Could it have been an hour or two?"

"No, it could not." He stared down at his folded hands. "I see that I must tell the whole story." He rubbed his thumbs together. "That was one of the days when I was suddenly taken with good resolutions. I passed by all the bars on the way as I went about my affairs, and there's not a bar on the way that I couldn't lead you to in a hurricane and a power failure. So it's sober I was when my doorbell went buzzing that evening. I knew who it was, and the mood I was in, I wanted no part of her. But *buzz buzz* it went, so at last I went and opened the door. And I saw—forgive me— that it was one of her seductive moods she was enjoying." He glanced up and down again. "The Lord forgive me, what I was seeing was not my old friend and"—a hesitation—"my sometime bedmate, but an ugly, fat, frowsy, blowsy old woman with a loathsome simper on her face." Another glance. "Rest yourself easy. It wasn't me who choked the life out of the poor creature. I couldn't have borne to touch her."

Martha made no comment.

"In the end, I'm ashamed to say, I slammed the door in her face. Full of resolution I was. Coffee was to be my drink from that time forward. I went to my stove, and coffee I made, and coffee I was drinking, sitting in my one and only easy chair and gazing into the future, finishing my second cup and thinking that coffee was all I'd be drinking for all time to come." A grimace. "There's a mistake. But those were my thoughts at the time, and it was in the middle of those thoughts that something at the window caught my eye, and there was the mysterious figger we're concerned with, light-foot and agile, all in black, running down the fire escape."

"While you were drinking the second cup of coffee."

"All I did, between sending Wilma on her way and seeing the feller come down the fire escape, was make that coffee—instant, it was—and set myself to drinking it. Even with the odd few minutes here and there for meditating on my sorry state, none of that could be taking me any more than half an hour at the absolute outside, for by the time I poured myself the third cup I was sick of the taste, so I opened up the cupboard once more and sweetened it with a dose of Irish." He raised his right hand. "Hi, my name's Frank, and I'm an alcoholic. But I can swear on the bailiff's Bible there was nothing but coffee in my mouth when I saw that fellow on the fire escape."

TWELVE

MARTHA KNEW Brooklyn Family Court by reputation: the crowd-control ropes and security guards, the swarming corridors, the assembly-line court calendars. Innumerable state judicial conferences had deplored the mess, but all proposed solutions had proved politically unacceptable.

She searched out the clerk's desk to record her appearance; then she took a seat on a bench outside the courtroom among a shifting cluster of humanity of every hue and form that could be found in the infinitely various city of New York—fretting babies, skittering small children, sullen-eyed adolescents, anxious-faced parents, lawyers and social workers with bundles of files under their arms—

All the same, it was a relief to be at work.

Having heard Francis McInerny out, she had feared he might change his mind and ask her to accompany him to a police station and stand by while he told his story. But he did not. He escorted her to the street and waited until she flagged a cab.

Digging for cab fare in front of her building, she had discovered the self-defense book at the bottom of her handbag. She had propped it open on top of the chest of drawers and tried a few of the exercises. The result was not particularly satisfactory. One needed a partner to simulate the assailant; defending oneself against air put one in constant danger of losing one's balance.

Eventually the court officer called the Oberfell case

and admitted Martha into Judge Harry Wallerstein's courtroom.

The Zables were standing with their lawyer at the front. Martha picked out Geraldine at once. The Oberfell sisters shared bone structure and body-fat distribution. Martha knew from the file that Geraldine was forty-six; it was a taken-for-granted forty-six, signaled by sensibly heeled shoes, a good wool coat over a knee-length wool dress, an outer-boroughs permanent, and redder lipstick than was generally worn in the city that year. The short broad-shouldered man in flannel slacks and sport jacket standing beside her, carrying a lined windbreaker over his arm, had to be Neil Zable.

The other man, tall and paunchy in a vaguely shabby navy blue suit, was unmistakably a small-time matrimonial specialist. He met Martha with the mandatory handshake and heard without perturbation her explanation of her appearance in Enid's stead. Kimmel, his name was, Maurice Kimmel, Maurie to friends of ten minutes' standing.

The judge peered over his half-glasses and said, "Why, it's Martha Patterson. What brings you here, counselor?"

They played out the mandatory recognition scene; then Harry Wallerstein became judicial, shuffling among the papers before him. "Bad business," he muttered. He peered down over his glasses. "My condolences. Very distressing."

Geraldine's, "Thank you," was barely audible. Neil nodded.

"Sad thing for a little girl to lose both her father and her mother." He became brisk. "Well, Mrs. Patterson, there isn't a lot to do now, is there? I take it you're here to consent to dismissal."

But Martha was determined not to impersonate a rubber stamp. "Not just yet, Your Honor," she said. "The assertion that my client is deceased is based solely on an affidavit of the respondent, Geraldine Zable. While I have no reason to doubt her statement, a motion to dismiss must be supported by the best evidence. That would be a certified copy of the death certificate." One must be punctilious as to the details or lose one's edge; the fact that careful lawyering would also prolong her contact with the Zables, about whom she was curious, was irrelevant.

Kimmel said, "Your Honor—"

"It isn't ready yet," interrupted Neil Zable.

Kimmel flapped his hand at Neil; the judge said, "Let your attorney speak, Mr. Zable." He looked at Kimmel. "What's holding it up?"

"I don't know, Judge. It could be the medical examiner or it could be the NYPD. Or I guess it could be the Health Department's computer." He shifted into argument mode. "Judge, if we put this motion off, the child's status could hang in limbo for months. Mrs. Zable is the deceased's sister. *Older* sister. She knew Wilma Oberfell since the lady was born. She's the one that made the identification the medical examiner is going to rely on. Judge, my clients and the little girl have been through the wringer for months. Let's get it over with and let everybody get on with their lives."

Nice job, thought Martha.

"I understand your argument," said Judge Wallerstein. "But I have to agree with petitioner's counsel. I'm not going to dismiss a mother's petition for custody of her little girl until I have official documentation that the mother is no longer with us. Official, Mr. Kimmel.

I'm going to adjourn this matter until you get the death certificate. How much time do you think you'll need?''

"YOU'RE MARTHA PATTERSON, right?" said Neil Zable. They were outside the courtroom once more. "You're the one that found her, right? So what's the malarkey about death certificates? *You* know she's dead."

Maurie Kimmel said, "Take it easy, Neil."

Geraldine said, "Neil." The skin around her eyes was puckered with distress. "I know you're just doing your job," she said to Martha.

"Sure she is," said Neil. "Dragging everything out and jacking up the fees, that's a lawyer's job." He wheeled toward the stairwell, nearly colliding with a young woman who was joggling a whining toddler in a stroller. "C'mon, Gerry. I got a job to get to sometime today."

Geraldine surrendered. Sending an apologetic grimace back over her shoulder, she edged through the crowd after him.

Maurice Kimmel shrugged. "God knows how it happened, but the kid's a sweetheart." He shot his cuff and consulted his watch. "Do you have time for coffee, counselor? My next case isn't on for another hour."

Ah. Maurie Kimmel was curious about Wilma's murder. Fair enough; Martha was curious about the Zables. She found herself, as well, seized with nostalgia for the clatter and garrulity of the coffee shops that inevitably appeared across the street from courthouses. "Yes," she said. "All right."

ENSCONCED IN A BOOTH, Kimmel said, "Terrible thing."

"Just so."

"You discovered the body?"

"I did."

"She was strangled?"

"So I'm told." She must enlarge her contribution to this colloquy. "It wasn't a pretty sight. Did Geraldine see her? It would be dreadful for a sister."

"Yeah. Terrible." Maurie Kimmel dumped two packets of sugar into his cup and stirred. "Any idea where the police are heading?"

"None whatsoever," she said. "They don't confide in me."

"Probably some junkie."

"Possibly. I understand her handbag had been rifled. But the TV was still there. I don't know about other valuables."

"From what Geraldine says about that apartment, I don't know how you'd tell. That was no place for a kid." He gulped coffee. "I honestly don't know why she wanted to rock the boat. It isn't as if she was really separated from the kid. She was at Geraldine's most weekends, when she wasn't pie-eyed. Geraldine paid for a cab. The kid called her 'Mommie' and she pushed her on the swings. I don't know why she couldn't let it go at that. No offense, but your client couldn't have handled being a full-time mother." He gulped coffee again. "It's a terrible thing to say, but maybe it's just as well. You know Harry Wallerstein. No offense if he's a friend of yours."

"Not to say a friend. I know him."

"Well, then, you know. Enid's good, I hope you know. She knows how to push his buttons. And between you and I, now it's over, I have to say Neil's mouth is not a lot of help."

"Wasn't a guardian *ad litem* appointed for the child?" asked Martha.

"We made a demand. Harry said he was waiting for the psychiatric before running up any more court expenses, but I happen to know he was holding off until he could get Josie Fleischer."

"I don't know Josie Fleischer," said Martha.

"Another blood-tie maven." Maurie Kimmel shrugged. "Our best shot was if she flunked the psychiatric. How did she do with the shrink?"

"I have no idea. It was Enid who observed. Tell me, would the Zables have been much upset if Wilma had won custody?"

"Devastated. Geraldine's had Rosemary since she was born. Wilma was totally out of it for over a year. They called it postpartum D, but the fact is, she wasn't too tightly wrapped a long time before that. If Wilma got the kid now, after all that, Geraldine would have been devastated. Not to mention the kid. Neil, too, for all his mouth."

"Has his business stood up to the recession?"

"I devoutly hope so, Martha. His retainer only covers 20 percent of my fee to date. It burns him that Wilma gets a free lawyer and he has to pay."

"You bill him for each court appearance, of course."

"Sure. Standard billing."

"And because you came in today without the death certificate, now you have to come back again when you get it."

Maurie Kimmel laughed. "You got to believe me, Martha, that's not my doing. I tell him we should wait for the death certificate. He says bleep the death certificate, Geraldine saw her sister lying dead in the morgue, let Geraldine tell the judge Wilma's dead. He's the client, so we go. Now we have to come back, the way I warned him, and *now* he's burned.''

Martha said, ''What's the hurry? They have the status quo.''

''They want to clear the decks so they can adopt the kid. Get her out of limbo.''

''Maurie,'' said Martha, ''you know that's nonsense. They can't start the adoption process without the death certificate anyway.''

Maurie Kimmel said, ''No comment.''

''It almost makes one wonder if money might be involved.''

''The father's estate? Peanuts, Martha. Thirty-five hundred, four thousand, something like.''

''Might there be undisclosed assets?''

''Not that I know, Counselor,'' said Maurie Kimmel, ''my clients have no ulterior motive in contesting this proceeding. They love the little girl as if she were their own, and they desperately want to continue giving her the kind of wholesome—''

Martha laughed. ''Save it for the judge, Maurie.''

''Plus Neil Zable is a pain in the butt with the patience of a flea.''

''Just so.'' Martha took a ritual look at her watch. ''I must get back. It's been a pleasure, Maurie.''

''All mine.'' He drained his cup and followed her.

On the way out, she overheard somebody say, ''TGIF.''

She had forgotten it was Friday. She had forgotten the Christmas party was that evening. She had forgotten to buy the gift for the unknown Family Law secretary.

She detoured, located a Hallmark shop, and found a coffee mug that said something complimentary about secretaries and came in a gift box.

THIRTEEN

BACK IN HER OFFICE, Martha opened the Brooklyn phone book to the business listings.

A-Z Appliances had a store on Avenue U in Brooklyn, one in Queens, and two in the near Long Island suburbs, all listed in the Brooklyn directory. She thought of an innocuous question and punched in the Brooklyn number.

Yes, said the voice that answered, they had Sunday hours, 10:00 a.m. until 5:30 p.m.

The Queens store also had Sunday hours.

Martha tried the first of the Long Island stores. After seven rings, an answering service told her that A-Z Appliances was "closed for inventory." The service had no information as to when the store would reopen.

The other Long Island number produced a strident trio of electronic tones and a robotic voice: The number she had di-aled was no long-er in ser-vice.

Maurie Kimmel might have a problem collecting his fee.

Her phone warbled almost as soon as she hung up. She answered, and a clear tenor voice said, "Good morning, Ms. Patterson. Brian Irish here." She had never heard of Brian Irish, but a conjecture began to form. "I'm an attorney representing Francis Mc-Inerny," he said. "He tells me he's also a client of yours, in a manner of speaking."

"What's your area of practice, Mr. Irish?" she said.

"Criminal," said Brian Irish.

"I see," she said.

"Could I persuade you," said Irish, "to clear your calendar enough to pay me a visit in aid of this mutual client of ours? I'm just up the street from you at 16 Court."

A calendar of wild horses, of course, would not have prevented Martha from paying Brian Irish a visit. They agreed to meet at one-thirty.

THE LAW OFFICES of Irish & Doyle were decorated in mahogany paneling and Oriental carpet. Ushering Martha into a conference room, Brian Irish explained that he and Frank McInerny were longtime friends—good-enough friends that Irish was willing to help McInerny through a tight spot for old times' sake.

"I'm relieved that he followed my advice," she said. "Has he talked with the police yet?"

"We're working out arrangements." Irish smiled. An adversary would be well advised to take note of Brian Irish's smile. "It seems you didn't tell Frank quite everything you know. It seems you discovered the body."

"That's correct."

"I'd appreciate hearing about that. Frank's knowledge leaves off the night before."

There was no reason not to repeat the story. And if she was to be of any use, she must include Detective Jamison's interview with Tessie Doone.

Irish said, "So the Doone woman heard Oberfell slam the door, but you found it unlatched. Frank must have left it unlatched when he was getting out of there after finding the body."

"Or producing it," she said.

"That isn't our theory. Frank says you talked with

Oberfell at the office that afternoon. What did she say?''

''Very little. She was looking for the person in charge.''

''What for?''

''She wouldn't say. She said she didn't know whom to trust.''

''Trust? About what?''

''I have no idea. I didn't know her at all. I should think Mr. McInerny would be in a much better position to guess.''

''What's your take on the mugging of the paralegal?''

Oh, dear. For an instant Martha was carried back more than six decades, pitched into the unwelcome role of playground tattletale. But McInerny was, however tenuously, a client; Carlos was only a coworker. She said, ''I thought Carlos's story had holes. On the other hand, each detail could have a perfectly innocent explanation.''

Irish said, ''Let's hear the holes and the innocent explanations.''

There was no help for it. ''He had a scrape on his head which he said he had suffered during the assault. It was still bleeding when he got to the office, but it seemed to me that the scrape was too superficial to be still bleeding to that extent. He'd had at least a twenty-minute subway ride, plus the time it took to go to housing court and then back to the office, since the injury occurred. Forty or forty-five minutes, at least.''

''You think he made up the mugging and scraped himself for verisimilitude?''

''I'll leave the conjectures to you. He might have

got the scrape as he said he did and rescraped it to impress Howard."

"Or maybe he's a hemophiliac."

"I doubt it. Hemophiliacs are greatly concerned about bleeding; Carlos was no more than inconvenienced."

"All right."

"He hadn't informed the police. He says he was both woozy and in a hurry to get to court. Again, one must allow that he has a point."

Irish nodded.

"He didn't notify the tenants of the theft until it was too late to stop payment. He says he telephoned Mr. McInerny and asked him to do so. Once more, that would be a sensible action. Mr. McInerny, however, says there was no call." She paused before continuing. "That need not necessarily mean that Carlos is lying. I suppose it's possible that Carlos delivered his message, but the answering machine failed to record. Mr. McInerny told me it's an old one."

"Mm. I'll see that it's tested."

"Or Carlos may have given the message to Wilma and she failed to pass it along. Mr. McInerny says she'd have left him a note, but no doubt you have noticed that people do not invariably do what one expects."

A fleeting smile interrupted Irish's concentration. He drummed a rat-a-tat on the table with the top of his pen, then said, "OK, devil's advocate for a minute. If this fellow Quinones did leave a message and Frank did get it, what would he have to gain by not notifying the tenants?"

"It might delay the stop-payment orders long enough to let the money orders be cashed," said Martha. "Carlos suggested that Mr. McInerny might have arranged the mugging."

Irish's eyebrows rose. "Cute. How did he play it out?"

"Well, he told me the muggers went straight for the portfolio in which he was carrying the rent payments, as if it were their principal goal, and took his wallet more or less as an afterthought. He suggested that Mr. McInerny might have told them where the money would be. He suggested that Mr. McInerny might be associated with an organization with the capacity to launder the money. He mentioned the Irish Republican Army."

"This Carlos Quinones," said Brian Irish, "is a very cute fellow."

"He's a first-rate housing advocate," said Martha.

"You're conflicted."

"I am. However, I suppose truth must be served. And in the service of truth, I must report that this was what Carlos said the second time I heard him tell the story. The first time the order was reversed; they took the wallet first and then the portfolio."

"Did he now?" A pause. "What does he look like?"

"Short, slight, substantially mustached. Have we got to the hooded figure on the fire escape?"

"I would dearly love to find somebody else who saw the hooded figure on the fire escape."

"What about the timing?"

"The Big Mac and fries?"

"The police told you about the McDonald's take-out?"

"Not the police."

"Who—oh. You've spoken with Enid Morgan?"

"About an hour ago."

Brian Irish had indeed been busy. "Well, then," said Martha, "to belabor the obvious, the man on the fire escape appeared too early. Wilma didn't eat at the McDonald's; she took the food home with her. Enid told me the autopsy showed that she had eaten it an hour or two before she died. So if someone killed her and then fled down the fire escape only twenty or thirty minutes after she went up to her apartment, she wouldn't have had time to eat and digest it to the extent the autopsy found."

"Frank thinks she'd have eaten as soon as she got on the subway. Or possibly she didn't die immediately."

"I shouldn't have thought one could survive a strangling and then die later," said Martha.

"Oh, one could. If you call it surviving. Lack of oxygen can put you in a coma, but the vegetative centers can hang on for quite some time. She might have hung on for several hours, still digesting, after the fellow went tearing down the fire escape."

"As in the right-to-die cases," she said.

"Time of death is vulnerable."

No doubt. It was his field, not hers. "I must mention something else," she said.

"What's that?"

"Mr. McInerny sent someone to my home with a message for me."

"Right."

"I don't think he is being entirely forthcoming about how he got my address. At first he said Wilma told him."

"She followed you home. She could have picked up your address off the front of the building."

"Just so. But he says the only time he saw her after that was when they were standing in his doorway that night after her psychiatric examination. And at that time they were quarreling."

"Maybe not all the time."

"Bear with me, please. At first he said she had told him; but when I asked him just when that was, he changed his story. He said Wilma hadn't told him word of mouth; she had left a note in his apartment."

"People do seem to change the stories they tell you."

"But he can't produce the note. He says he lost it."

"Not surprising, where he is."

"Just so. But he seemed evasive."

"He's four days into recovery. People do strange things. But thanks. I'll follow it up. What else should I know?"

A-Z Appliances?

No. Martha knew too little to talk about the Zables. "There's nothing else I can think of."

"You hesitated. What was it?"

She shook her head and smiled. "Nothing, Mr. Irish."

FOURTEEN

THE CHRISTMAS PARTY was gearing up. Casseroles and salad bowls crowded the tables that had been pushed together at the back of the library; the bar table was loaded; a boom box was belting out a salsa beat; the West Brooklyn staff, plus husbands, wives, significant others, and kids, clotted the room.

Martha circulated for a time, exchanging enough agreeable inanities to appease her social conscience. She avoided Carlos. Presently she spotted Howard and John in conversation at the far end of the room and made her way across to them.

She had met Howard Wallace in the early seventies. A thirty-year-old law student camouflaging a 1960s social conscience with a corporate haircut, Howard had misled a Reilly, Whitman interviewer into taking him on as a summer intern. (He claimed, when questioned about the incongruity, that he wanted to find out how the enemy operated.) He was assigned to Trusts and Estates under Martha's supervision.

The preservation of capital being about as far from Howard's convictions as could be found, the assignment could have produced rancor. What actually happened was a bonding between the two anomalies. The forty-eight-year-old token woman and the thirty-year-old ex-hippie took to eating brown-bag lunches on financial-district benches, debating social values, music, and the Marx brothers. By the end of the summer the roles of supervisor and intern were only marginally significant; they had become comrades.

Howard went on to finish his law degree, enlist in the trenches of poverty law, marry, beget, and divorce. His hairline receded as his waistline, reputation, and responsibilities expanded. Martha, meanwhile, began to press the firm for a wider role; she took on some bankruptcy practice and a few Social Security disability cases, volunteered to coordinate the firm's pro bono offerings, and was ultimately appointed to the pro bono committee of the Association of the Bar of the City of New York.

Now Martha was in some sense the intern and Howard was the supervisor. It made no difference.

Howard welcomed her to a satiric monologue on the governor's budget proposals. John, she noted, was less than absorbed. He kept looking over his shoulder toward the door. A few minutes later, he peeled off and crossed the room to where a young woman had appeared in the doorway. With great interest, Martha watched him lay an arm across her shoulders, brush a kiss on her cheek, and steer her across the room.

"Martha Patterson," he said, "this is Sunny Searle."

Martha made only a token attempt to disguise her scrutiny; it was expected of her, and Sunny was doing some scrutinizing of her own. She was interested to note that John, so spectacularly good-looking, had taken up with a woman who, though entirely presentable, was in no way remarkable to the eye. Sunny Searle was solidly boned and muscled; her jaw was square, her mouth wide and mobile, her light-lashed eyes an indeterminate sort of hazel. Light brown hair was held by a clip at the nape of her neck and fell below her waist.

"How do you do, Sunny," Martha said.

They exchanged a no-nonsense handshake, and Sunny said, "It's a pleasure to meet the renowned Martha Patterson."

Not at all displeased, Martha said, "Thank you."

John said, "By way of orientation, Martha, Sunny runs an outfit called Welfare Advocates Organization that does more for clients in a week than we do in a year."

Thus cued, Martha said, "Tell me, please, what the Welfare Advocates Organization is."

Sunny said, "An organization that advocates for welfare recipients."

It appeared to be the unserious answer to unserious inquiry. The depth of Martha's interest was being tested. She said, "May I ask what that translates into, day by day?"

This triggered the serious answer. Welfare Advocates Organization did Fairhearing representation, battered-women counseling, family-planning referrals, college financial aid advice, workshops in English as a second language, and parenting skills and job-readiness. An AA group met on Tuesdays and Fridays, NA on Wednesdays and Saturdays.

Howard, to whom it was surely familiar stuff, excused himself.

Martha, to whom it was not, asked about funding. Sunny spoke of diminishing government aid, a corporate sponsor, trickles of individual contributions, volunteer workers. "It's a scramble," she said. "Time you want to be spending helping people, you're spending on a money chase."

"And I suppose it can only get harder," said Martha.

Sunny turned her eyes to the ceiling as if seeking divine guidance. "If they do what they say they want to do..." She looked at Martha and heaved a mighty sigh. "We all know the system isn't what it should be, but...welfare to work? Without *any* kind of program for preparing *completely* unskilled people—and where are the jobs, anyway? Oh, don't get me started. Please. It's a Christmas party; joy to the world."

"Deck the halls," said John. "God rest you merry, gentlemen. Listen, I have to go and check on something. Why don't you get some food, and I'll see you in a while?"

Martha watched Sunny's eyes follow him across the room. When he had disappeared into the corridor, Sunny turned back to Martha. "Did he tell you about his big churning lawsuit?"

"He did," said Martha. "What's going to happen when the restriction on Legal Services class actions takes effect?"

"Joy to the world." Sunny sighed once more. "Well, Martha, let's take his suggestion and get some food."

Sunny seemed to know nearly everyone on staff, so it took them a while to get to the food line. Once there, she prevailed on Anita, who seemed to be a particular friend, to stop hovering and join them. They balanced plates on their knees, perched wineglasses on bookshelves, and gave themselves over to eating.

Dancing had started in the middle of the room when a commotion at the door drew Martha's attention. She looked over and saw standing in the doorway a skinny old man with a straggly beard. He had on a stained canvas coat with grimy sheepskin collar and cuffs;

dirty corduroy trousers, torn at one knee, were rolled over broken work boots; matted gray hair straggled down his neck below a ripped astrakhan hat; his face was smudged as if from huddling over a smoky fire in an oil barrel. He was stooping under a bulging trash bag slung over his shoulder.

A homeless man with his load of returnable cans, peering into the loud brightness of their party.

"Who's that?" said Anita.

The ghost of Christmas present, thought Martha, a chill brushing her skin.

He ventured a few limping steps into the library, and Martha heard Sunny whisper, "Oh, my God."

Somebody near them said, "How'd he get up here? I locked the elevator."

"Clients will find a way," said somebody else, and took a step toward the doorway.

But Howard had already detached himself from the crowd and was advancing across the room. "Yes," Martha heard him say to the man at the door, "what can I—"

"*Mer*-ry *Christ*-mas!" called out the bag man. His cracked voice filled the room.

Howard drew back a step, the beginning of a smile creasing his cheeks.

More heads turned. Talk dwindled. Somebody turned off the boom box and the dancers grew still.

"*Mer*-ry *Christ*-mas, everybody! Huh-huh-huh." The bag man's head jerked in time with a parody of a chuckle. "Huh-huh-huh," he said. "Huh-huh-huh. Huh-huh-huh." He shuffled to the middle of the room and eased the bag off his shoulder to the floor. "Mer-ry Christ-mas. Have you all been good little girls and boys?"

"I don't believe this," said Anita.

It was John.

He bent over the trash bag on the floor, fumbling with his gloved fingers at the plastic ties. Succeeding at last in loosening them, he reached in and lifted out a gift-wrapped box and turned it to read a tag.

JOHN DID NOT break character, even at close range when people advanced to receive their ten-dollar-limit gifts. He handed out all the presents, picked up the empty trash bag, peered into it with an air of bewilderment, and then bundled it under his arm and shuffled out of the library, disappearing up the corridor.

Twenty minutes later he was back, out of costume and cleaned of makeup, eating sparingly from the plate on his knees and accepting compliments, riding the high of the actor at curtain call.

Anita said, "John, that was gross." She shook her head. "No, that isn't what I mean. Not gross. I mean—" She flung out her hands, at a loss.

"Disconcerting," said Martha.

"That's it," said Anita. "It makes you—think."

Carefully quartering a meatball with the side of a plastic fork, John looked at her and smiled. "Thank you."

Martha said, "You must have had stage training."

"My disreputable past," he said, casting a glance at Sunny.

Sunny said, " 'Time present and time past…' "

" '…are both perhaps present in time future'? God forbid." He forked the fragment of meatball into his mouth.

Anita said, "I don't see why you're so antsy about

it. That conference where we did the role-playing? You were so good, you got us all into it.''

''Role-playing?'' asked Martha.

''Something my predecessor set up,'' said Sunny. ''A weekend conference to try to create a liaison among welfare recipients, advocates, and caseworkers.''

''It was heavy-duty stuff,'' said Anita. ''We had workers playing recipients and recipients playing workers—*that* was worth watching. Guys playing girls and girls playing guys.''

''You actually got civil servants to participate in this enterprise?''

Anita laughed. ''Sunny, remember that AOM from the Bronx?''

''AOM?'' asked Martha.

''Assistant Office Manager,'' said Anita. ''She was playing a recipient once, and she got so mad she almost punched out''—she stumbled—''whoever…whoever it was playing the worker. She was something else. Remember her sitting around with us afterward in that bar and telling us how you could rip off the system?''

''Good lord,'' said John. ''I'd forgotten that.''

''John, how could you forget? I can still see you sitting there beside her at that big round table back in the corner, egging her on.''

''How irresponsible of me,'' said John.

''That was a great weekend,'' said Anita. ''I learned a lot from it.''

''You learn from everything, Anita,'' said John. ''But it made no impact on DSS that I've ever seen.''

THE MUSIC got louder; the conversation became more raucous and less coherent; people began to writhe about the cleared space in what now passes for dancing. Perceiving that she was growing curmudgeonly, Martha detoured to leave her gift in her office—a coffee mug that said I'm Not Old, I'm *Really* Old—and took herself off in a taxi.

Saturday she gallery-hopped. Sunday she went to Alice Tully Hall with friends and listened to Beethoven's late quartets.

FIFTEEN

THE HEAT hadn't come up by the time Martha left for court on Monday morning. Anita Pagan was sheltering in a garishly patterned out-at-the-elbows cardigan. On the whole, Martha would have preferred the sweatshirt, but it was nowhere to be seen, and by the time she returned, the office was warm and the cardigan was hanging on one of the hooks by the door.

She found John in the front corridor, distributing the mail. This task, although ostensibly assigned to the office manager, was in fact undertaken by anyone wanting to kill a few minutes after the postman had deposited the bundle next to the mailboxes.

"How'd it go?" asked John.

"Adjourned until Friday," she said. "Someone was supposed to bring the welfare case file to court and didn't."

"Is the stay continued?"

"Oh, yes. The judge was annoyed with the Department of Social Services."

"Good."

"And the landlord's lawyer was annoyed with everyone."

"To nobody's surprise. If DSS is being fractious, you'd better be prepared for oral argument. And by the way, are you free for lunch?"

As she was announcing her acceptance, a phone warbled. John listened for a moment, said, "Excuse me;

that's mine," laid down the bundle of mail, and went off up the corridor.

Martha picked up the bundle. Perhaps Tessie Doone had received Cousin Kevin's affidavit from Philadelphia and dropped it in the mail. A frivolous notion, of course.

The mailboxes were in alphabetical order, with two exceptions: Howard Wallace had three boxes, already half-full, at the left-hand end of the row, and Martha's single box stood like an afterthought at the right-hand end. It was still empty.

Half of Howard's mail was official correspondence. The rest was junk; a greeting-card-shaped envelope without a return address, hand-addressed in large, round handwriting, for example, was surely a fundraiser disguised as personal correspondence.

Martha got nothing. It was absurd to be disappointed.

"I HOPE THIS JOB is working for you," said John.

They had gone to a modestly upscale Moroccan place on Atlantic Avenue. The decor was plush, the ambience quiet, the prices surprisingly moderate.

"Very well indeed," said Martha. Caution impelled her to add, "So far."

He smiled. "God knows we need you. Especially now."

There was an invisible Martha behind the aged crone who appeared to the world's eyes—a Martha who was twenty-eight years old and responded instantly to the smile. The visible Martha, on the other hand, was entirely aware of the ludicrous spectacle presented by old women who succumbed to the charms of good-looking young men. This Martha was on her guard. Doubly so, for this good-looking young man was an actor as well. Martha was acquainted with three or four actors. Nothing in that acquaintance had dispelled her conviction that whatever one's age, no good is likely to come of succumbing to the charms of an actor.

In any case, although the matter was of academic interest only, this actor was taken.

John asked, "Is the staff treating you OK?"

"Quite well," she said, "to the extent they deal with me at all. Luther Young seems hostile, but I suspect that's his style. Even Howard seems to handle him kid-glovishly."

"You don't know the story?"

She raised her eyebrows.

"Titled 'How Howard Wallace became project director of West Brooklyn Legal Services.' ''

"All he told me was that there was a vacancy about six months ago and he was selected to fill it."

"That's a seriously laundered version."

"And now," she said, "you will air the dirty linen."

He laughed. "Since you insist. A mess preceded the vacancy."

"A common sequence."

"Inadequate supervision, shoddy legal research, sloppy accounting. Statutes of limitation were missed; winnable cases were lost; funds were commingled. I wasn't here at the time, thank God. I was a simple staff attorney in the Bronx."

"Was the office sued?"

"Legal Services clients don't commence malpractice suits. It was Anita and Luther who blew the whistle. You have to hand it to them. They could have been whistling themselves onto the unemployment line. Anyway, after an incredible amount of shouting and arm waving, headquarters finally shoved the project director into a research position in Central Office and assigned Howard to West Brooklyn. He persuaded two middle management people to resign and arranged for half a dozen union members to get dispersed around the city to offices that didn't especially want them and that they didn't especially want to go to.''

''I take it you replaced one of the purged management people.''

''Howard knew me from a clinical program I took in law school. I thought I might be cutting my own throat, but I couldn't pass up the promotion, plus the chance to trade the South Bronx for Brooklyn Heights. I live at Seventy-sixth and Columbus, so all I had to do was take the downtown Number 3 instead of the uptown.''

''Have you run into hostility?''

''Well, I don't exactly have most-favored-nation status with L and T. They had the idea Luther should become project director. But it's manageable.''

''What about the Family Law Unit?''

She hit the nerve she'd been aiming for. He flushed and made a business of taking a drink of water. ''You mean Enid,'' he said. ''That isn't political. We used to date. As you may have noticed, it didn't work out particularly well. She was in the GBU when I got the call, so I'd have been supervising her, and I actually considered turning the job down. But she managed a transfer into Family Law. Where,'' he added after a moment, ''it looks as if she's found her niche.''

Martha said, ''You seem to be doing all right with your own unit.''

''Oh, GBU gets along fine. Victory was a new hire in September, so she's mine. Gwen comes in, reads medical records, wins her hearings, and goes home. Orlando gets off an acid remark from time to time, but he doesn't really care who's running the show as long as his check arrives. And of course Anita's grateful that all she has to do now is keep sticking it to DSS.''

Martha smiled. ''She isn't alone in that.''

The single eyebrow. ''It's that obvious?''

''Perhaps there's another story.''

''I guess you could say so,'' he said. A pause. ''I was a welfare child.''

Surprised, she said, ''One would never guess.''

''My father was an alcoholic. You live and die keeping up appearances.''

''Ah. Just so.''

''He drove his car into a tree when I was eleven. His blood alcohol count got in the paper. My mother made it out to be a onetime shot of bad luck, but that was about her limit. His life insurance ran out in short order, and she just couldn't play the hand she was dealt. She was brought up to be a wife.''

''Oh, dear.''

''She should have remarried, but she had some idea, God knows why, that it wouldn't be fair to me. She got sick whenever it was time to go for a job interview. We nearly got evicted before she could make herself go apply for welfare. Now I realize it was depression, but what does a kid know? My father was dead and my mother was sick, so obviously it was up to me.''

''Were you the only child?''

''Little Johnnie, the man of the house. Paper routes in grade school and after-school jobs in high school. Plus dealing with the welfare office.''

''Where was this?''

''Cleveland. I'll say this for young Johnnie. It took

him about five minutes to scope out the system. Shabby but clean, and don't ever look as smart as you are. I took a lot of pride in keeping the checks coming in.''

"I'm sure.''

"And of course nobody was to speak the *w* word. We fostered the myth that my father had left a small estate and I was eking it out with my after-school earnings.''

"And thus you learned to act.''

"God, I was *on* twenty-four hours a day. The senior class play was a piece of cake compared to real life. When I got to Yale, I hung out at the drama school, and then I moved to New York and took some more acting classes.''

"Yale,'' said Martha. "On scholarship, I assume.''

"Tons. Financial aid, loans, jobs. My high school guidance counselor was a winner. If there was money out there, she found it.''

She. The actorly charm at work. Martha smiled.

John might have read her mind, for he smiled back before continuing. "I knocked around with an improvisational group, street theater and Tribeca clubs. One summer in stock, and then the company went belly-up. There wasn't any money in it, but my mother'd remarried when I went to college, a guy who turned out to be another alky, and she OD'd on sleeping pills when I was a junior, so I only had myself to consider.''

"Dear me. I'm sorry.''

"Accidental, they decided. Eventually I got sick of serving power lunches to Wall Street lawyers between auditions for jock-itch commercials, so I took the LSAT and went to Columbia.''

Yale and Columbia Law. Ivy League all the way. And it showed; he could have occupied any office in

Reilly, Whitman without raising eyebrows. "But you didn't go to Wall Street after all," she said.

"One summer clerking for Cravath settled that. Then I met Howard, and it came together."

"You found your niche?"

"You know that case of yours where the minor is working and they're trying to count her earnings against the welfare grant?"

"Tessie's niece. Yes."

"The same thing happened to us right after I got my working papers. I thought the world would end. I was sure we'd get evicted. But I'd learned to read the fine print, and there it was, the right to representation, with a phone number for Legal Services. I didn't even waste a call. I walked in, scared out of my skull, and they gave me to a paralegal, one of those matriarchal black women, you know the type? Victory'll be one when she grows up." He smiled. "Barbara Dobson. She took about ten minutes, total, to listen to my story and look at my papers and make three phone calls, and I fell in love. Now I'm practicing poverty law and Barbara Dobson gets five pounds of Godiva chocolates every Valentine's Day."

SIXTEEN

THE PHONE WARBLED as Martha reentered her office after lunch. She picked it up and television gabbled in her ear. *"Hello,"* she shouted. *"This is Martha Patterson."*

"Oh, yeah, Miz Patters. Wait a minute, I turn it down."

Shifting the phone from hand to hand, Martha slipped out of her coat and hung it on the hook behind the door. The TV hushed. She sat down at her desk, opened the bottom drawer, and tucked away her handbag.

A clatter announced Tessie's repossession of the phone. "Yeah, Miz Patters. That letter you want, from my cousin? Kareem can bring it over now, that OK? An that stuff for Vibelle's Fairhearin, I got that, too."

"Isn't Kareem at work?"

"He work Saturdays, he get Mondays off."

"Very well. I'll be here until five o'clock."

IT LACKED only fifteen minutes until five when her phone gave out the intercom tone and Gloria, the receptionist, announced Kareem Hewitt to see her. Martha was reading John's brief. It was an impressive piece of argument; whatever had gone wrong during his all-nighter had obviously been corrected.

She set the brief aside and went out to collect Kareem.

Neat in clean chinos and an open-collared shirt, he

was quietly passing the time of day with Gloria. His short, powerful build and high-rise haircut were less threatening here in the West Brooklyn milieu. He got quickly to his feet, snatching a small backpack from the floor and his ski jacket from the back of his chair. Somewhere he had learned to give a solid handshake.

One normally engaged in a little small talk on the way to one's office. *Are the police still hassling you about Wilma's murder?* Hardly. She took refuge in the generic. "How are things going?"

"Going good," he said. "I got myself into college."

"Your grandmother mentioned that."

"I took a couple college classes upstate, and I aced them." They turned into her office and he took a seat in the client chair. "We had this newspaper, where I was. I got to writing stories for it, like I got started writing, I couldn't stop. We had this particular teacher, a guy writes TV scripts, says I can handle college. High school, forget it; I was cutting all the time, into stuff you don't want to know about." He opened his backpack and pulled out a manila envelope. "I got what you said."

The envelope held two packets. One consisted of a much-worn copy of Vibelle's birth certificate, a current report card, and a bundle of pay stubs. Martha nodded and laid it aside. She slipped the rubber band from the other packet and unfolded a sheet of paper that was folded around a bankbook.

To Whom It May Concern:
    I, Kevin Hill, being duly sworn, do hereby state that all the money in my account I used to have in the Freedom National Bank of Philadelphia PA is my own money from my accident and not one

dollar of it belong to my Cousin Mrs. Tessie Doone until such time as I die. The only reason I put Mrs. Tessie Doone's name on the account was because I want it to go to her without no lawyers in case something happen to me. I never wanted for that money to make problems for Mrs. Tessie Doone and I have took her name off of the bank account and put the money away somewheres else in just only my own name so she can go on getting her SSI checks which she don't have nothing else to live on. I am putting the old bank book with her name on it in with this to show I took the money out.

It had been notarized in Pennsylvania.

The bankbook had been punched through with perforations spelling CANCELED. She opened it.

A joint account in the names of Kevin Hill and Tessie Doone had been opened with a deposit of $10,000 in June, three and a half years previously. The first withdrawal had been made on the thirteenth of August of that year. It was followed at roughly bimonthly intervals by withdrawals of amounts ranging between $150 and $300. A withdrawal of $500 had been made in the previous July; in the five months since then the withdrawals had been larger but more irregular. The balance of $2,343.61 had been withdrawn and the account closed on December 11.

She looked at her calendar. Today was December 11. She picked up the affidavit again. It had been notarized December 11. She looked at Kareem.

"What I did," he said, "seemed like I better talk to Cousin Kevin face-to-face, you know? Be sure he know what we need. I took a bus down to Philly, just got back to the Port Authority. This OK?"

Well—yes. On the face of it, it was OK. Between them the affidavit and the bankbook touched all the bases, and Kevin Hill's presence would not really be required at the hearing.

"Something wrong?" asked Kareem.

She said, "Not really. It's just that live witnesses are always best. How old is this Kevin Hill?"

"How old?" She heard in his voice the mistrustful raising of back hairs, like a dog's muttered growl. "I don't know. He looks like an old man, all crippled up like he is, but him and Gran are close, so I guess maybe he's around her age. But he's near as crippled up as she is. He can't get on no bus and come to New York."

Martha was not to be intimidated on her own turf. She smiled. "In that case, Kareem, we must give the judge a mental picture of him. The judge must have a good basis for believing an absent witness."

The back hairs settled. Kareem said, "Yeah, well. I see what you mean."

"What kind of accident was it that crippled him?"

A moment of silence. "You wanna know the truth, I don't know Cousin Kevin that good. It's Gran and him is close. You should be asking her this stuff."

"I see," she said. "Very well, I'll call her."

"Yeah, that's the way. She can tell you all about him." He shifted his weight. "Excuse me, this place got a men's room?"

"Just next door," she said. "I'll go make copies of these, and I'd appreciate it if you'd wait a few minutes before you leave. I need to check with my supervisor in case there's something else we'll need."

Her mind worrying at Tessie's case, Martha nearly

ran into Carlos Quinones, who was just passing her door, apparently on his way to the men's room. He flashed his smile and said, "Hey, Martha."

Jagged thoughts about bleeding scrapes and telephone messages scratched at her consciousness. "Hello, Carlos," she said, trying to match the insouciance of his smile, and hurried on to the front.

A secretary was finishing a copying job, the last pages just emerging into the collating bins. She showed Martha how to reload the paper trays; like all office machines, this one had idiosyncrasies. Fanning a ream of paper, Martha reflected that learning how to reload the copier was another step toward establishing one's acceptance in an office.

"LOOKS GOOD TO ME," said John. "Am I missing something?"

She said, "Look at the dates."

He turned pages.

She said, "Tessie said the robbery to which Kareem negotiated a plea was something over three years ago, which is more or less when the account was opened."

"Mm."

"The regular withdrawals seem to have been made during the time he was incarcerated, the biggest one was made about the time he was released, and the others have been made since he was released."

"Mm. Yes."

"The account was closed and the affidavit was notarized this morning. Kareem went to Philadelphia, he says to make sure Cousin Kevin got it right."

"You still think Kevin Hill is Kareem what's-his-name and the original deposit represents his take from the robbery."

"I want your opinion."

He flipped through the pages. "There are three-letter codes beside the withdrawals, but I don't see any guide to what they mean." He tossed the bankbook back on the desk. "So for all we can tell, Tessie might have made those withdrawals by mail."

"I wonder if the bank could produce the record," said Martha.

"I don't know."

"And whether the Social Security Administration will investigate the possibility."

"Good question. But look here, Martha, it still wouldn't have been Tessie's money. It would have been Kareem's, and even if Tessie did make the withdrawals, she would simply have been administering the funds for Kareem's benefit. It shouldn't affect her SSI."

"But in that case, the money isn't Kareem's either. It belongs to whomever he robbed. So if Tessie were to say that Kareem was cousin Kevin, and the money was really Kareem's, mightn't it affect his parole? Surely the authorities would want it back."

"Mm." John picked up the bankbook once more and tapped it against his thumb.

"I suppose I must warn Tessie that a further investigation is possible."

John nodded. "Give her a chance to avoid perjury, if such is her present intention."

"Although I doubt if she'd choose to avoid perjury by informing on her grandson."

"Yes, well." He handed the bankbook back to her. "Let's not swim that river unless we fall in it. And look, Martha, now that the account's been closed, the money's no longer even technically available to her.

She could reapply and get back on SSI from this time forward, if she's willing to let the retroactive go.''

''Just so.''

''Although they might try to recoup the overpayment.''

''Oh, dear, so they might.''

KAREEM WAS STANDING in the doorway to the rear stairs, two doors beyond her office, smoking a cigarette and blowing the smoke into the stairwell. As she approached, he stubbed out the cigarette on his shoe sole and let the door close. She gave him back the originals; the copies would stay in her files. He dropped the dead cigarette butt in her wastebasket, tucked the papers in his backpack, picked up his jacket, and accepted her escort out to the waiting room.

Back in her office, she picked up the phone and dialed Tessie's number. She got a busy buzz and hung up.

SEVENTEEN

IT WAS PAST SIX-THIRTY when Martha finished tracking down an elusive point of Medicaid law. Howard's door was shut, but light showed through the crack underneath.

In the street, the wind tossed flecks of coldness against her face. Christmas lights had been glittering in store windows since Halloween. They had seemed tawdry, but now, with snowflakes fluttering, the glitter all at once became festive. "God rest you merry, gentlemen!" she found herself caroling, under her breath, to be sure, "let nothing you dismay—"

Edwin, she thought with a pang.

But Edwin had loved her bursts of lightheartedness. She ordered herself to accept this gift of the spirit. "Joy to the world!" she sang, just audibly to herself. No one was likely to hear her with the wind whipping around their ears; if they did—God rest you merry, gentlemen!

She bypassed the subway station at Borough Hall and turned west through Brooklyn Heights, down to the Esplanade. There, while traffic on the Brooklyneens Expressway roared invisibly below her feet, she stood at the rail and gazed across the East River through the intermittent snowflakes at the light-spattered masses of the financial district, an alternative star-spangled sky set on edge, the clichéd magic land of Manhattan at night.

Beautiful, one exclaimed; then, uneasily, one added,

*from this distance, with the filth and anger and despair
hidden by distance—*

That, too, a cliché.

The financial district. Money. Martha Patterson
among the ficus trees; Wilma Oberfell dead on the floor
among dusty cartons; Kareem Hewitt's armed robbery;
Kevin Hill's vexatious bank account. A derelict with a
garbage bag full of gifts.

God rest you merry, gentlemen, let nothing you dismay.

Eventually her feet grew too cold to be ignored. She
turned back and walked briskly the four blocks to the
subway entrance.

She had used her last token that morning. Waiting
in line, she pulled off her gloves and tucked them into
her coat pockets, turned back the flap of her handbag,
and reached for the zipper of the compartment where
her billfold traveled.

It was unzipped.

With a stab of anxiety, she slid her fingers into the
compartment. Her heart lurched; it was empty.

Nonsense. She must have put her billfold back into
the wrong compartment after paying her lunch check.
Twenty-eight years old and distracted by an actor.

Methodically, she probed the depths of each compartment.

No billfold.

The line moved up one. She clamped the handbag
under her arm and felt in her coat pockets. They held
only her gloves and a crumpled tissue. Unbuttoning the
coat, she tried her suit jacket pockets, where she found
a dime change from the coffee pool and another tissue.

She stepped out of line and rummaged through the
handbag once more.

Her billfold was gone.

She ordered her quivering nerves to calm down. Her keys had not been taken, nor her checkbook. Her driver's license was still in its separate compartment. The credit cards could be canceled. As for the cash, there was more where that came from. Not at once, of course; the ATM card had been in the billfold, so she would need to wait until a bank opened. But for tonight, she could take a cab and borrow the fare from the doorman at the end of the trip.

And then, climbing back up the subway stairs, she thought that perhaps it wasn't gone at all. Mightn't it just possibly have slipped out into the bottom desk drawer where she stowed her handbag while she was in the office?

It wouldn't hurt to look. She turned the corner into Court Street and headed back through the snowflakes.

From the street she could see light in the corner windows on the fourth floor. The front door of the building was locked. Through its inch-thick glass, she could see the lighted elevators standing open. She found a button on the door frame and pressed it. Minutes passed. Nothing happened. Not until she had pressed it again, harder and longer, did she remember that John had said there was no night porter.

She stripped off her gloves and groped in her handbag for keys. The lock was at the bottom of the door; it operated a vertical bolt seated in a metal footing embedded in the concrete sill. She squatted, her knees complaining. The key gritted into the lock but refused to turn. She jiggled it, twisting left and right. At intervals headlights slid over her, deepening the shadow on the keyhole. A couple of pedestrians scrunched past.

This was absurd. She would find a cab and check

her desk drawer tomorrow. And get a replacement for the faulty key.

It stuck when she tried to withdraw it. She gave it another irritated jiggle and suddenly it turned, the bolt grated up, and the door moved a sluggish quarter-inch on its hinges.

She worked the key loose, struggled to her feet, and pushed through. Inside, she balanced for a moment between obligation and preference. She ought to relock the door behind her—she was reluctant to engage in another struggle.

Ought carried the day. She knelt on the cold marble of the entryway and reinserted the key. This time she found the effective jiggle after only four tries, and the bolt snapped to. She got to her feet, crossed the lobby, and stepped into a waiting elevator. The ''4'' button was locked. She sorted through the keys to find the smallest, unlocked it, and ascended.

One ceiling fixture lighted the waiting room. The elevator closed and started back down as she crossed to the door to the back area. It gave way to a third key. The corridor lights were still on, and as she crossed to the corridor off which her office opened, she heard the distinctive sound of a file drawer sliding shut. Turning the corner, she found Howard peering out of John's office. ''Martha!'' he said. ''What are you doing here?''

His going-to-pot figure and balding head eased a tension of which she had been only marginally aware. She said, ''I seem to have mislaid my billfold. I came back to see if it might have slipped out of my bag into a desk drawer.''

''Oh, lord,'' he said. ''Let's hope.''

He accompanied her back to her office. She switched on the light and pulled open the drawer.

It was empty. She had known it would be empty. She pushed it shut.

"How much?" asked Howard.

"About two hundred." The figure, so far beyond any walking-around money her recently acquired clients would carry, embarrassed her. "One likes to be prepared to take cabs."

"So what do you think happened?"

"I was careless," she said. "There was a client in my office—a client with a criminal record, no less. He went to the men's room and I went to the copier, leaving my bag in the drawer." Her dismay was not solely for the loss of her billfold. Cousin Kevin notwithstanding, she had begun rather to like Kareem Hewitt.

"Who is he?"

"His name is Kareem Hewitt. Actually, it's his grandmother who's the client. He was bringing in some documents for her."

"Want to notify the police?"

She hesitated; and as she did so, a new memory assailed her.

Howard said, "What is it?"

"Carlos."

"Oh, God."

"Just so. He was coming down this corridor when I was on my way up to the copier."

"It's the way to the men's room," said Howard.

"I'm aware of that."

"The fact is, you could be invaded by anybody."

"Just so. It seems to me a police inquiry would be more disruptive than helpful. Unless you think otherwise."

"It's up to you," he said.

"I think I should let it go. Please excuse me for a few minutes. I must call my credit card service."

WHEN MARTHA STARTED back up the corridor, she found Howard in front of an open file drawer in Anita Pagan's office.

"Howard," she said, "what are you looking for in our files?"

He looked up. "Do you know anything about an Armbruster case? Jolene Armbruster?"

"It isn't mine. Why?"

"Somebody asked about it, and I can't find it on the computer."

"Do you need the answer tonight? Why not circulate a memo?"

He pushed the drawer shut. "I'm not sure I want to go public. It was a strange communication." He switched off the light and herded her out of the office.

In the corridor, she stopped being herded. "Howard," she said, "what's going on?"

"Going on?"

"Don't stall, Howard, it doesn't become you. I heard Carlos's yarn about the mugging, you know. Then I listened to Wilma say she was looking for somebody to trust. Then I found her body."

After a moment he said, "Yarn. Good word."

She waited.

"This is confidential," he said.

"Then perhaps you shouldn't tell me."

"No, I think you're entitled. I don't know the ramifications, but somehow that so-called mugging came to the attention of somebody responsible for prosecuting organized crime."

"He did report it?"

"By phone, finally. The yarn seemed to have some dropped stitches, so they went after him. He's a gambler, Martha."

"I saw him going into OTB one day."

"I think he probably goes into OTB every day. My predecessor habitually gave him advances on his paycheck. I discontinued the practice. He hits his colleagues for loans and they shell out. He's well liked."

"Just so."

"But it wasn't enough. It never is. He got into the hole with a loan shark."

"That's what happened to the rent?"

"I expect he got concerned about his kneecaps. The checks and money orders were cashed. The police tracked them through a bent bank officer. And it seems they already had a hidden camera on the loan shark's door. It had picked up Carlos going in with that portfolio."

"No knives."

"It seems not."

"What's going to happen to him?"

"I don't know yet. Listen, Martha, I'm relying on your famous capacity for reticence."

"Howard," she said, "do you think Wilma Oberfell found out? She had a habit of following people around."

"Is that right?" Howard was silent for a long time. "You're asking if I think Carlos did her in to silence her."

"I'm afraid I am."

"No. Larceny to save his kneecaps, yes. The way he'd see it, he'd only be ripping off our insurer. But murder to cover the larceny no. Not Carlos." He reached for his back pocket. "God, I'm sick of this stuff." He hauled out his wallet and took out two twenties. "This should get you home."

"That isn't necessary, Howard. I can borrow from the doorman."

He took her hand and folded it over the bills. "Don't argue."

It would save her from explaining to Boris. "A loan," she said. "Thank you." She unzipped her handbag yet again, thrust the bills deep into the inner compartment, and zipped it shut.

EIGHTEEN

MARTHA'S FESTIVE SPIRIT had gone the way of her billfold.

The prospect of exchanging even a perfunctory, "Good evening," with Boris repelled her. She was in no frame of mind for *Pride and Prejudice,* nor for anything that might be on television, nor for any of the movies Edwin had so persistently purchased. The only friend she felt like telephoning was in Minneapolis, immersed in the task of installing a sculpture exhibition. Calling her son and daughter-in-law in California was out of the question—it was three hours earlier on that coast; she'd get the sitter or one of the children, and fond as she was of her ten- and twelve-year-old grandchildren, at that moment she lacked the patience for youthful self-absorption.

In any case, she shrank from laying out over the telephone the absurd and slightly frightening situation in which she found herself. She had planned to relate her adventures at a suitably relaxed moment during her Christmas visit. That was more than a week away.

No doubt food would improve her mood. She turned west to the coffee shop where she had sparred with Harris Gordon. After broiled breast of chicken and the house salad, she walked. After she walked, she went home and had another go at the self-defense book. She longed for a sparring partner; kicking someone would feel good.

She slept fitfully and the next morning arrived at the

office forty minutes late, having stopped at her bank
for cash. She pulled a half-sheet of paper from her
mailbox and read:

To: Staff
From: Howard
Date: Tuesday, December 12

This is another reminder to keep valuables under
lock and key. We've had another theft, this one
from an unlocked desk drawer.

John came to her office shortly after she had settled
to work, dropped into the client chair, and said, "The
way we're abusing you, I'm surprised you keep coming
in."

"Howard told you of my negligence?"

"Now, Martha. That's called blaming the victim and
it's an absolute no-no in poverty practice. I hear Carlos
was in the critical neighborhood."

"Howard told you?"

"Professional courtesy. Luther had to be told and
I'm his equal in rank."

"I wish he had waited a bit," she said. "There's
always the chance that I mislaid the billfold at the restaurant when we had lunch. I must call them when they
open."

John's expression became abstracted. After a moment he shook his head. "You put it back in your
bag."

"You saw me do that?"

"We had separate checks. You took out the exact
amount for your bill and tip while we were still at the
table, and then you put your wallet back in your bag

and zipped it before we got up to go to the register." Half a smile. "I was thinking that somebody playing Martha Patterson would have to deal with a restaurant check in exactly that way."

Not sure whether to feel complimented, she said, "Even so, it's by no means certain that it was Carlos who took it."

"Howard made that clear. It doesn't matter all that much. Your wallet is the least of his troubles."

She said, "What's going to happen?"

"I don't know. Luther's still arguing. I've got to prep for that Eastern District argument in the morning, so I cast my vote and split." He ran a hand through his hair. "We'll know by the end of the day. There's a board meeting tonight, and Howard wants to announce a *fait accompli*."

IT WAS HARD to identify any particular source of discomfort. Perhaps there was a bit more clustering around the coffee machine than usual, or perhaps it was simply her own uneasiness. She ate lunch by herself, several blocks away at the Greek storefront. After lunch Anita brought her a handful of new cases. Their conversation was limited to a discussion of the issues presented. Martha's caseload was now up to fifteen.

Late in the afternoon, John appeared, dropped into her client chair, and said, "Carlos is out."

"Fired?"

"Persuaded to resign." Lines around John's mouth showed how his face would age. "Howard is some kind of interrogator."

"Carlos admitted he'd taken the rent?"

"He didn't deny it. He gets a month's paid leave and silence unless a prospective employer asks specifically why he left.'' He rubbed his hand across his face. ''Do I really want to be a project director when I grow up?''

He did, of course, but before she could formulate a response, Enid appeared in the doorway. She raised her level dark brows at John. ''So you've canned Carlos.''

''What did I tell you?'' John said. ''Speed of light.'' He got to his feet and slipped past Enid into the corridor.

Enid said, ''I just got a call from Wallerstein's chambers. They've got the death certificate. He'll put it on at two on Thursday if you want to appear; otherwise we'll stip.''

Martha consulted her desk calendar. There should be time to get to family court after Tessie's Fairhearing. ''I'll appear,'' she said.

''What's the story with your wallet?'' asked Enid.

''It vanished,'' said Martha.

''I heard you told Howard that Carlos took it.''

''Not quite. Gossip simplifies the complex. What I actually told Howard was that Carlos was in this corridor while my office was unoccupied.''

''That'd be enough for this rumor mill.''

''Just so. However,'' Martha said, striving for fairness, ''Carlos wasn't the only one with the opportunity. A client was in my office as well. He did excuse himself to go to the men's room and smoke a cigarette while I was out of the office, but I suppose he'd still have had time to explore my desk drawers.''

''Late in the day?'' said Enid. ''Around five? Short stocky black guy?''

Martha nodded.

''He wasn't pissing and smoking the whole time. I saw him cruising the halls back in Family Law.''

And that, of course, gave Carlos even more time than she had supposed to rifle her desk unobserved.

As she was contemplating the implication, Howard glanced into her office. Since she had no desire to talk with Howard just then, it was just as well that she wasn't his quarry. "Oh, there you are, Enid," he said. "Do you have a couple of minutes?"

Enid said, "Sure," and they went off toward her office.

WHEN MARTHA LOOKED at her watch again, it was six o'clock. In the waiting room, Howard was chatting with three or four people gathered around a tray of sandwiches on the receptionist's desk. John was at one end of the room talking with a woman in jeans and sweatshirt; Luther was at the other end talking with a man in slacks and sport jacket. The board of directors, mandated by law to include representatives of the private bar and of the client population, was gathering for its monthly meeting.

Not, thank heaven, Martha's responsibility.

NINETEEN

IN NO HURRY to return to her empty apartment, Martha stopped in a presumptively French restaurant for dinner with a half-bottle of wine. It was after nine when she took her mail from the boxes by the elevator. She sorted through it on the upward trip. Among the brochures was a greeting-card envelope addressed in large, round, neat handwriting to Ms. Martha Patterson. The Christmas card season was under way.

She hung up her coat and hat, dropped the brochures into a wastebasket, lighted the stove under the teakettle, and slit open the envelope with a paring knife.

It wasn't a card; it was a letter. A genuine letter, handwritten in blue ink on lined paper. The writing was neat, round, and so large that the writer had skipped every other line. It was a penmanship that had been taught in the schools of the fifties. Some women—only women, no men—still wrote that way in maturity. A niece of Edwin's wrote like that, which may have accounted for the sense of déjà vu Martha was experiencing. But this wasn't from Carolyn.

The kettle whistled. She poured the boiling water over a tea bag. While it steeped, she began to read:

Dear Ms. Patterson,

I hope it's all right to call you "Ms." I did see that you were wearing a wedding ring, so maybe you'd rather be called "Mrs.," but I know you're a professional woman, so I decided the best thing is to call you "Ms." I hope that is all right. I am writing to you because I have found out some things really wrong going on and I just don't know what to do....

Martha turned to the last page. There, above two postscripts, was the signature "Wilma Oberfell."

She fished the tea bag from the mug and stirred in a teaspoon of honey, carried mug and letter to the living room, and propped herself against the back of the chaise lounge.

...just don't know what to do. There is stealing going on. I guess somebody might think stealing from the "system" doesn't really hurt anybody but when you stop to think about it, "stealing from the system" is stealing from people too. I was very sick for a long time when I had my baby, and I needed the "system" or I just don't know what would have happened to me. I would probably be sleeping in one of those cardboard boxes on the street. The thing is, I don't know whom to talk to, because I know people on the inside don't want to "blow the whistle" on each other, but I do think somebody should know about this. I don't want to put any more than this in writing. I have just got to talk to somebody, and I think with you being new in the office I can trust you to look into it and not cover up for people. I'm afraid you think this is sounding "paranoid," but if I can just get through this awful psychiatric examination so I can get my little girl back I need to talk to you and tell you what it is I've been finding out, and when you look into what I tell you I don't think you will think it is paranoid. I wish I could find out your home telephone number because I don't feel like it's really safe to call you at your office. I know how people can listen in on switchboards. I hope you will "get in touch" with me some way, and I know when you do you will "listen."

Very sincerely yours,
Wilma Oberfell

P.S. I did want to talk to the head of your office, because he is somebody who needs to know what is going on if anybody is going to do anything about it, but it's very hard to "get in touch" with such a busy man.

P.P.S. Please don't tell anybody about this letter, because you don't know whom I mean and you might talk to the wrong people. I don't want to put down any names in writing.

Martha's first connected thought was that this letter had been shuffling around in the postal system for more than a week. She picked up the envelope and examined the postmark. It had been mailed in Brooklyn on December eighth.

Friday. Four days after Wilma had been killed.

Was it a forgery?

Both substance and style sounded like Wilma. The letter writer knew how to use *whom*.

Martha supposed the letter could have lain uncollected in the bottom of a mailbox for four days, but it was more likely that someone other than Wilma had mailed the letter. One might postulate a ghost—the unquiet spirit of a murdered woman seeking to tidy up unfinished business. Intellectually, Martha had never altogether ruled out the possibility of more things in heaven and earth, and so forth. Who knew what might lie, so to speak, on the other side of the force that binds the atom? But one explored the mundane first, and as a consequence one never seemed actually to have to invoke the supernatural.

Postulate, then, that someone had found the letter and dropped it in the mail last Friday. Martha looked at the envelope again. It had her street address but not her apartment number. There was no return address. She turned it over. She had slit the top in a single clean cut, not disturbing the flap where it was stuck to the body of the envelope. The flap was stuck down unevenly.

She stretched to hold it directly under the table lamp.

The flap was stuck down off center, and it was rippled as if it had once been wet. Such might be the appearance of an envelope that had been steamed open and resealed.

Martha had once handled a probate that involved a forged will; the case had taught her that fingerprints could be lifted from paper. If someone had steamed open the envelope, then that someone had surely handled the letter itself. The letter paper might well bear fingerprints.

When Wilma had addressed this envelope, she had known Martha's name and street address. West Brooklyn Legal Services did not give out home addresses. Therefore, Wilma had addressed it after she had followed Martha home.

But she had left it unmailed. Where? In her apartment? In the rifled tote bag?

Wherever she had left it, someone had found it. And someone seemed to have steamed it open, read it, resealed it, and then, four days after it was written, mailed it. In Brooklyn.

The letter must go to the police, of course, but first she must show it to Howard. The buck stopped on Howard's desk.

TWENTY

MARTHA SLEPT BETTER than she had expected but not as well as she would have liked. She awoke for good at a quarter to five.

She spent half an hour with the workout tape and another quarter of an hour in the shower; she prepared cooked cereal; while it simmered she dissected half of the grapefruit that lurked in the refrigerator. With all that, she was ready to go at a quarter past six. So she walked. The snow had stopped, but clouds still sat halfway down the World Trade Center towers to the southwest. On the Brooklyn Bridge, serenely bounded and enlaced by its perfectly proportioned towers and cables, the screams of gulls wheeling over the white-flecked gray expanse of the East River just managed to penetrate the whining tires of inbound traffic. Wind whipped her coat about her knees.

She arrived just after seven-thirty. The waiting room was fully lighted but empty. The door into the office area stood ajar. The corridor lights were on. All the Landlord-Tenant offices were dark, but she was pleased to see light spilling from the corner office. John's light was on as well.

A smoky odor scratched at the back of her nose; it smelled like the Fourth of July. Had the board meeting concluded with fireworks?

She turned toward Howard's office.

Behind her, she heard a door open; John's voice called sharply, "Martha! Wait!"

She turned and saw him coming in through the back-stairs fire door. His face was white, the skin stretched taut over the bones.

"What is it?" Alarm edged her voice. "What's wrong?"

"Howard—" His voice caught and he cleared his throat. "Somebody broke in. Howard's been shot."

"Howard?"

"He's..." John cleared his throat again. "He's dead."

Dead? Howard?

She looked over her shoulder at the light pouring from the corner office. The movement dizzied her and she reached out to brace a hand on the wall. Through white noise roaring in her ears she heard John say, "Martha!" She felt his hands grasp her upper arms, and then there was a supporting arm around her shoulders. She let him guide her a few steps, heard him say, "Sit down," let herself sink into a chair. She heard from a great distance, "Put your head down," and felt hands press on her shoulders. She submitted, resting her forehead on her knees.

She was dreaming again, of course; she had drifted into one of those useless spells of slumber she had been slipping into and out of all night.

She felt her handbag slide off her arm and heard it thump on the floor.

She became aware of discomfort. The weight of her arms hanging at her sides dragged her shoulders forward; her back ached. She raised her hands to cradle her forehead on her knees, and gradually the world steadied. The roar moved out of her head and separated into the hiss of rising steam in the pipes and the thrum of traffic outside.

"Are you all right?" John's voice was distinct now and close by.

Not a dream.

She raised her head. The world stayed steady.

She was in John's office, in the chair beside his desk. Gray light crept through the big windows, challenging the fluorescent lights. Steam hissed in the radiator. Outside, traffic whirred and a car honked.

John's look of concern embarrassed her. She sat up straight and said, "I'm all right." Her mind was clearing as rapidly as ground mist under a rising sun. She groped for her handbag and laid it in her lap. "Howard," she said.

John rolled his own chair out from his desk and sank into it. "The door's jimmied." He jerked his head toward the corridor. "The door from the waiting room."

She hadn't noticed it. "I just saw that it was open."

"The lock's split out of the frame."

"You came on in?" But recalling her own foolish entry into Wilma's unlocked apartment, she said, "Yes, of course."

"I saw Howard's light from the street. I thought he was already here."

Howard. Impossible. "You're sure he's dead?"

"God, yes."

"Have you called the police?"

"Not yet." A wry twist of the lips. "I made it to the can in time to dispose of my morning coffee. And then I saw the fire door wasn't all the way closed, so I—God, Martha. The dumb stuff you do when you're in shock."

"You went to look on the back stairs?"

"I was rattled. I guess—I don't know. Did I think I'd go up against an armed addict with acting-class karate? Eventually it dawned on me that I was being a world-class asshole, and as I was coming back in, I saw you heading up there toward Howard's office. I didn't want you to see it, so I shouted.''

"Thank you," she said.

"It's time for a sanity fix," he said. She watched him reach for his telephone and punch in 911.

THE SENSE of dreaming kept drifting back.

They went out to the waiting room, on the way looking at but not touching the splintered door frame where the lock had been wrenched loose.

Martha's body seemed molded of heavy clay; she could do no more than sit inert on one of the waiting-room chairs. John couldn't sit still. He had been wearing a topcoat; he took it off and slung it over the back of a chair. He was wearing a splendidly tailored suit of charcoal worsted. He paced, ran his hand through his hair, and massaged his eyes. "If I still smoked," he said, "I'd be smoking."

"That smell," she said. "Like firecrackers. I suppose it's gunpowder."

"I should have called 911 as soon as I smelled it."

"You knew?"

"I had a part in a mystery once. My character had to shoot a revolver. I went to one of those downtown places and took lessons."

After a while she said, "Did he stay after the board meeting, or did he come in early?"

"I don't know. He was going to meet me early, but he did stay sometimes when his work got backed up." He paced to the elevators and back.

"You're here early," she said.

"The TRO's on today. He was going to run me through the fact statement."

Then she remembered; the preliminary argument in federal court, seeking a temporary order restraining DSS from cutting off the named plaintiffs' grants, was on this morning's calendar. The charcoal worsted was explained.

"You're early, too," he said.

"I didn't sleep well." She heard a distant siren. "They're coming."

He stopped pacing and looked at her. "You've done this before." He drew in a breath. "I feel unrehearsed."

She said, "I thought improvisation was your forte."

After a moment he said, "That was a dumb crack, wasn't it. This is no performance, Johnnie; this is your life." He dropped into a chair and rubbed a hand across his forehead. "The whole damn thing seems so unreal."

"Shock," she said.

The siren sounded directly below. "My mentor," he said. "Oh, shit." He lowered his face into his hands. Outside, the siren died. She saw his shoulders move with a sequence of deep breaths.

She heard the right-hand elevator begin to move. John got to his feet and threaded his way between the chairs to face the elevators. The door rolled open to admit two police officers hung about with radios and nightsticks and holsters. They seemed, in that familiar space, larger than life-size. One was black; one was white; both were male.

Martha stayed in her chair, a lump of clay still, inert except for her brain, which suddenly seemed hyperactive. John was the one to recite the facts. He was composed now, though still as pale as parchment, standing erect, balanced evenly on both feet, his head tilted back to make eye contact with the taller cops. He did well, his shaken emotions by that time well wrapped. Martha's skittering mind threw out the image of a terrier addressing two much larger dogs—a boxer, perhaps, and a Doberman. The same species, different breeds. The big dogs listened, making no excess motions, nodding now and then.

Then the older one, the white, went through the jimmied door with John, back to Howard's office to view the actual site of this rupture in the fabric of the universe. The black one, the courteous Doberman, stayed with Martha, addressing her as "ma'am" and asking if she was all right.

Yes, she said, yes, thank you; rather shaky but all right; it's a shock, naturally. He said Yes, ma'am, it certainly must be, and made sure he had her name right in his notebook. His radio burst at intervals into crackles and sputters. He went over to the broken door frame and examined it, moving the door to and fro with the end of his pen.

"How many people work here?" he asked.

Martha knew, but her mind took a moment to produce the facts. "Eighteen lawyers," she said. A jolt to the solar plexus. "Seventeen now."

"Yes, ma'am," he said.

She ran her mind around the corridors, mentally peering into offices. "Seven—six or seven paralegals," for should she count Carlos? "Two investigators. Office manager. Secretaries—" She wasn't sure. "Seven, I think." She looked across at the desks: "Receptionist and switchboard operator."

"So thirty-some-odd people are going to be piling in here."

Plus clients. She pushed up her sleeve to consult her watch. It was just past seven forty-five. "The office opens officially at nine," she said. "Some come in early, depending—" She stopped herself from babbling. "There'll be clients as well."

And then they heard the steady tread of the other cop coming back and the lighter counterpoint of John's steps. John came through the doorway first, deathly pale, the lines of stress distinct around his mouth; then the policeman, his big body filling the doorway, his footsteps suddenly muted as he crossed the threshold from the vinyl flooring onto the mud-colored carpet. He looked across at his colleague and nodded and said, "Yeah."

TWENTY-ONE

MARTHA KEPT EXPECTING Howard to appear and demand an explanation for all the disruption.

The fourth floor was declared a crime scene, off-limits to all but the police. The startled super, summoned from the depths, was persuaded to unlock a vacant office on the fifth floor. The detective who did the interviewing left Martha with a uniformed officer while he questioned John behind the closed door of the inner office. Waiting, she had time to arrive at what she hoped was a rational decision. Wilma's letter was in her handbag; she must produce it. But tiptoeing along the outer limits of the Canons of Ethics, she judged that before she gave it to the police, she had a professional obligation.

She hoped Howard's admiration for her *famous capacity for reticence* was not misleading her.

Luther Young arrived as the detective was ushering John out. His scowl masking shock, he protested the shutdown of the office. Court appearances were calendared; client interviews were scheduled; emergencies would walk in. John backed him up.

They negotiated a compromise. Attorneys with court appearances would be escorted to their offices to pick up their files; all other business would have to wait.

Luther left to join the police officer who was intercepting the staff at the building entrance; John went down to the fourth floor to collect what he would need in court; the detective ushered Martha into the inner office.

She thought she would have no trouble remembering his name. He was sharp-angled, quick-moving, fast-talking; his name was Sharpman. He was solicitous but thorough. After the wide view—her relationship with Howard Wallace, her position at West Brooklyn— came the immediate facts: When had she arrived at the office? What had she seen, heard, smelled? What had John said? What had he done?

Then Howard himself. Martha's acquaintance with Howard had not extended very far into personal matters, but she was able to tell Sharpman that he was several years divorced, had two grown children, lived, as far as she knew, alone. A lover? She didn't know. Parents, siblings? She didn't know.

It occurred to her to wonder if anyone would be sitting shiva for Howard. Then she wondered if he would have wanted anyone to.

She asked a question of her own. "Was he shot? John stopped me—"

"Just as well," said Sharpman. "It looks like a shooting. Pending the autopsy."

"A break-in gone wrong?"

Detective Sharpman had rather a nice smile. It partly made up for his failure to answer. He asked about enemies.

Enemies?

Without pleasure, she told about the disappearance of the rent money and the coerced resignation. It was an old-fashioned word, *tattletale;* nowadays they would call her a snitch, wouldn't they? She did not express these thoughts to Detective Sharpman; the police cultivated and cherished snitches. Surely John would have told him anyway. Surely Sharpman would hear the story a dozen times today.

She told him about Kareem, Carlos, and her billfold. Sharpman said, "You didn't report it?"

"At the time I judged it would be more disruptive than productive. This"—lifting her hand in an inclusive gesture—"changes the emphasis."

"Mm-hm. Anything else?"

She took a deep breath, felt it catch in the middle, let it out. "Perhaps John told you. This isn't the first death."

He nodded and took her through the Wilma Oberfell affair.

In particular, he wanted to nail down two facts: that it was after Carlos had reported the mythical mugging that Wilma had turned up looking for someone to trust; and that Carlos, standing not far away in the waiting room, could have heard Martha tell Enid about Wilma's visit.

Finally, as she began to suppose they had finished, Sharpman said, "What brought you in so early this morning?"

She managed to avoid hesitation. "I woke up early."

"Any particular reason?"

A sigh came easily. "I'm recently widowed," she said. "The office is better than the apartment."

Sharpman's nice smile took on a sympathetic tinge.

RESTLESSNESS LED HER to take the stairs down. Not the back stairs behind the fire door just beyond her office; she took the front stairs. The fire door at the ground-floor level discharged her into a deep alcove beside the elevators, the front doors just visible beyond its mouth.

Two uniformed officers intercepted people entering

the building. On the sidewalk, a television camera was trained on a reporter who was tilting a microphone up and down from Luther Young's mouth to hers. Martha detoured around rubberneckers. A few minutes' walk brought her to the featureless stone box that housed the U.S. District Court for the Eastern District of New York. She passed through the security scanner and turned to the telephones.

Brooklyn Directory Assistance gave her Francis McInerny's number. Another quarter and five rings brought his answering machine. She told the tape her name and, after a moment's hesitation, her home phone number. Another quarter produced Manhattan Directory Assistance, whose robot voice produced the number for St. Honoria's Shelter. A fourth quarter brought a human voice that said Francis McInerny might be at a meeting that evening. Again Martha left her name and home number and used the word "urgent."

Then she consulted the wall directory, rode the elevator, and turned down a wide empty hall past several sets of imposing double doors.

Ahead of her, one of them opened and discharged a straggle of people. First came a man Martha did not know, suited and briefcased; then Anita Pagan and Victory King, dressed for court, and three other women whose best clothes showed still the shabbiness of poverty. Just behind them came John in the splendidly tailored charcoal worsted, the topcoat draped over the arm that held his briefcase. Behind him came two more lawyers, who shook hands all around and went off past Martha to the elevators.

The appearance had obviously concluded.

John looked ill and exhausted, but Anita was smiling and Victory was grinning. The unknown man with them was introduced as John's cocounsel, from a Legal Services office in Queens.

Martha asked how it had gone.

Victory said, "Great!"

The cocounsel said, "So far so good."

John nodded.

The judge, they told her, had ordered interim assistance; while the lawyers prepared their final briefs, the plaintiffs' families could eat, after a fashion, and maintain roofs of a sort over their heads.

Victory said, "It's a shame you missed it. John was so great. I can't *believe* Howard didn't show up."

Martha looked past her. John shook his head. They must have come straight to the courthouse from home, and John hadn't told them.

"BUT THAT'S INCREDIBLE!" said Victory. "I mean… he was so cool!"

John, muttering about an obligation somewhere, had hurried off toward the subway. The cocounsel had gone to retrieve his car for the trip back to Queens, taking with him the two Queens clients. The Brooklyn client had gone to the bus stop. It had been left to Martha to tell them, standing on the walk in front of the courthouse.

"He looked sick," said Anita. "I thought it was nerves. Well, I guess it was. My God."

Victory said, "What do we do now?"

"Go back and see when they'll let us in," said Anita. "This is unbelievable. Martha, are you OK?"

"I doubt it," said Martha. "I feel all right, but I suspect that's an illusion."

"You could go home."

"I'd rather be among all of you."

Victory said, "I know what you mean," and so the three of them proceeded down Court Street.

From half a block away they could see police cars still pulled up in front of the office building. They were in front of a coffee shop. They looked at one another and admitted to a mutual craving for coffee.

Others had had the same impulse. Clustered at pushed-together tables at the rear were, among others, Enid and two paralegals from the Family Law Unit; a Landlord-Tenant lawyer; Gwen Doherty, the disability expert; and the office manager. Chairs were pulled around. Surprised to find herself with an appetite, Martha ordered a Danish.

She was a celebrity. Their questions, though less orderly, were quite as comprehensive as Detective Sharpman's.

Victory said, "And John had to go to court after all that. I don't know how he did it."

"The show must go on," said Enid. She looked at Martha. "So what are the odds it was your client who pulled the trigger?"

"My client?"

"The black guy with the record. I told you he was prowling around Family Law yesterday. He could have been casing the joint."

"Enid, that's disgusting," said Victory. "A young black man walking around minding his own business, why is it you right away think he's a thief and a murderer?"

"Statistics," said Enid.

"That's absolutely disgusting," said Victory.

"Why is it you're assuming he was minding his own business?" said Enid.

Martha said, "With the fourth floor off-limits, I don't suppose you know if anything is missing."

"Oh, stuff is missing," the office manager said. "The police took me around."

"And all from Family Law," said Enid. "My little TV and Irene's laptop and the unit's Dictaphone, for starters."

"Weren't they locked up?"

"He had a crowbar," said the office manager.

Reaction-induced frivolity boiled over. "He?" said Martha. "Why is it that when someone breaks and enters and murders, you assume it was a he?"

"There you go!" said the Landlord-Tenant lawyer, who was male.

Enid looked startled. Then she laughed, and then, as if on cue, the women in the group cried, loudly enough to draw stares from other customers, "Statistics!"

WHAT MARTHA WANTED to do next would be easier if she had Wilma Oberfell's file. Lacking it, she had to negotiate for help.

Fortified by the coffee and Danish, she made her way through the security checks of Brooklyn Family Court to Judge Harry Wallerstein's chambers. The judge, to her relief, was sitting. His secretary, glad to be of assistance, looked up the name and phone number of the psychiatrist who had conducted Wilma's court-ordered examination.

I'm behaving crazily, Martha told herself, still giddy with reaction. *Obviously I need to talk to a shrink.*

She found a phone booth and dropped in a quarter. A quiet contralto that identified itself as belonging to Olivia Ullbright answered the third ring and said, "Oh, yes,'' when Martha identified herself as cocounsel on Wilma Oberfell's custody case.

The case was as dead as the client, of course, said Martha, but she needed to discuss one or two matters by way of clearing up the file. In person, please. She was in luck. Olivia Ullbright's five o'clock client had canceled. Fifty minutes would be available, at no charge to either Martha or the court.

Shrinks, thought Martha, *must experience quite as much curiosity as ordinary folk.*

The next task required a copy machine. She rejected the ones in the courthouse; in her experience, they were in permanent need of toner. In the branch library she made two copies of Wilma's letter and the envelope. Then, with a guilty sense of enforced truancy, she went off to restore her spirit in the American wing of the Metropolitan Museum of Art.

TWENTY-TWO

OLIVIA ULLBRIGHT lived on the fourteenth floor of a well-kept building on the Upper West Side. The doorman found Martha's name on his list of expected visitors and directed her to the elevator.

The psychiatrist was a short, round woman wearing an ankle-length caftan patterned in a subdued paisley. A braided coronet of graying light-brown hair coiled above a round-cheeked face, its good humor given character by attentive hazel eyes. Martha judged her to be in her middle fifties.

She showed Martha to a comfortable armchair in a small living room decorated in Asian style. "Judge Wallerstein notified me that she was murdered," she said. "He wanted to forestall my billing the court for a report. What do you need to know?"

Martha was no longer sure what she had come for. Well, this was a shrink; confusion was permissible, possibly even desirable. "Now that I'm here," she said, "I'm not sure I know."

Olivia Ullbright smiled with professional encouragement.

Martha said, "I discovered her body, you know."

"I didn't know. That must have been disturbing."

"Just so. I had met her for the first time only the day before. She wanted to talk with me—a stranger—about looking for someone to trust. But we were interrupted before she came to the point."

"Unfinished business."

"Very much so."

"Someone to trust," said Olivia Ullbright. "Interesting."

"Did she say anything about it here?" asked Martha.

"No. I suppose she could have been concerned about sounding paranoid in the context of a psychiatric examination."

"Is that significant?"

"I'd say so. She was able to exercise judgment as to whom she mentioned it to." Amusement curved the psychiatrist's lips. "Just what information is it you need to close out the file?"

Martha found herself returning the smile. "I'm afraid I equivocated. On mature reflection, I believe you ought to bill me for this hour."

"You are concerned with your own state of mind?"

"This morning—" She broke off as the sense of dreaming returned. "Dr. Ullbright, I'm seventy years old and incorrigibly middle-class. I'm not accustomed to the lurid."

Again the gentle amusement. "We might examine the preconceptions bound up in that statement."

Martha felt herself relaxing. "Just so." She drew a breath. "Last night the director of the office where I'm working was murdered."

The amusement faded.

"He was a friend. Equally to the point, it was he to whom Wilma wanted to confide her mistrust in the first place. He wasn't in the office when she appeared. I happened to be there instead, and so, in a manner of speaking, I became his surrogate. I recognize that my state of mind is confused."

"It's bound to be."

"Please"—Martha tried to keep an edge of desperation from her own voice—"can you tell me anything that might cast light on any of this?"

The shrink had the decency to respond directly. "Possibly. I did have the impression she was concealing something."

"Something that she didn't trust somebody about?"

"Possibly. She seemed to be suppressing excitement. It may have had to do with money. She seemed quite confident that she'd be able to support Rosemary, and I detected a kind of...slyness I suppose is a good-enough word...in that expression."

"Did she give any indication of where that money was to come from?"

"What she verbalized was the likelihood of getting her old job back. She had been a civil servant before her depression became disabling. But her affect didn't seem consistent with anything as prosaic as a civil service job."

"Might she have been anticipating a windfall?"

"That's an interesting suggestion. Was there a windfall in her future?"

"I don't know. Did she talk about Rosemary's father?"

"We explored the relationship. She had felt cheated by his illness and death. She was aware that she had fantasized an idealized family relationship—mommy, daddy, and baby—which had never come to pass. Did she have money coming from him?"

Martha said, "I've been told by the lawyers for both parties that Rosemary inherits between three and four thousand dollars from him. The child's legal guardian would presumably be the trustee of the funds."

"I had the impression that this windfall we're hypothesizing was to be a secret, even from her lawyer.

She turned away from the one-way glass and lowered her voice somewhat when she spoke of supporting the child.''

"Actually," said Martha, "I was thinking of something a good deal larger than four thousand dollars and something that wouldn't appear in the probate file. If that's what was on her mind, I'm sure she would have been reluctant to let anyone know there were material considerations in the effort to get the child back. Perhaps even her lawyer."

Olivia Ullbright said, "Mm."

Martha said, "Assuming this inheritance existed, I've wondered if the Zables also knew about it." Olivia Ullbright looked quizzical. Martha said, "Neil Zable appears to be a hostile man, and his business appears to be in trouble."

"You're suggesting—?"

"That he might have known about this legacy of Rosemary's and wanted to ensure that he and his wife would retain custody."

"To the extent of killing Wilma?"

"I believe," said Martha, "you've given me permission to entertain the lurid."

"You say 'Neil.' What about his wife? The sister."

"I've met Geraldine. Even with permission, my mind has trouble entertaining that notion."

Olivia Ullbright smiled.

"Of course, either of them—or both—would have had to suppose they were likely to lose custody of the child. I shouldn't think they'd engage in such a desperate action otherwise."

"Well, they may have been. Likely to lose custody, I mean."

"You found Wilma fit to be a mother?"

"There was the history of depression, of course, and she had an active fantasy life, but I found her well able to distinguish between fantasy and reality. She was an intelligent woman, and she was generally capable of exercising her intelligence. And Judge Wallerstein was sitting on the case."

"I know him," said Martha.

"It's a troublesome thought," said Olivia Ullbright. "The child in the custody of her mother's murderer. Tell me, how does the idea of a secret inheritance connect with Wilma's wanting to confide in the head of your office?"

Martha closed her eyes and leaned her head back against the cradling upholstery of the armchair. All at once her mind seemed scrambled. She became aware of Olivia Ullbright's waiting silence, opened her eyes, and said, "It doesn't connect, does it?"

"Something is disturbing you."

"Wilma seemed to be mistrusting someone in the office."

"You feel a loyalty to your coworkers."

"I've been there only a week and a half. But, yes. I like many of them, and I…honor the work they do." She took off her glasses and rubbed her eyes. "Now Howard's getting killed has muddled the whole matter of loyalty."

"Muddle is unpleasant," said Olivia Ullbright. "Particularly for somebody with highly developed intellectuality."

"Indeed."

"But sometimes it's a way of avoiding something more unpleasant."

Martha put her glasses back on. "Thank you very much."

A small smile. "And sometimes a muddle is simply a muddle."

"Resulting from a lack of crucial facts." Martha reached for her handbag on the floor beside her chair. She still didn't know what she had come for; the consequence was that she didn't know whether she had gotten it. "Dr. Ullbright, you must bill me."

But Olivia Ullbright said, "No, Ms. Patterson. My treatment room is back there," indicating a hallway leading deeper into the apartment. "This room is where I indulge myself."

TWENTY-THREE

MARTHA MADE HER WAY to Broadway and headed downtown toward the Seventy-second Street IRT stop amid the noisy complexity of the Upper West Side. The cold air was welcome against her face.

John lived in this neighborhood. She hoped he had managed to get some rest.

A couple of blocks down Broadway she passed a McDonald's.

Passed it, stopped, then masked her sudden halt by gazing into a florist's window.

What would be the point?

Never mind. Her time was her own. She turned back. She seldom ate anything McDonald's produced, but as a rule the coffee was tolerable. And hot. She joined the shortest of the three lines that snaked back from the registers.

The place was crowded with a polymorphous West Side clientele: whites, blacks, Asians, and Latinos, many with children. This being the West Side, there was also a Character. At a table near the counter sat a woman dressed in bag-lady layers, her hair dyed a screaming orange, her deeply wrinkled face so extensively made up that she might have been a clown on break from the Big Apple Circus, which was playing just down the street at Lincoln Center.

A brisk ''Next; what can I get you?'' from the round-cheeked girl at the register retrieved Martha's attention. She ordered a coffee.

The girl punched the register. "Anything else?"

"Nothing else, thank you. But—"

Do it.

She smiled, for one must not let this efficient young woman suppose that one meant to do anything so antisocial as register a complaint. "Could you tell me where I might find the manager?"

The efficient young woman was not at all put out. Raising her voice a notch, she called, "Mr. Vance."

A man in shirtsleeves standing behind the shoulder of one of the order takers looked up.

"Lady to see you. Seventy-five cents, please." Looking past Martha, her hand out to receive Martha's single, "Next; what can I get you?"

Mr. Vance came out from behind the counter. The coffee and the change appeared; Martha took them and stepped out of the way.

Mr. Vance answered her question with brisk patience and a shake of his head. "You see what it's like. Nobody has time to notice any particular customer. Unless there's something special about them. In a wheelchair, maybe, or like Madonna there—" He glanced toward the henna job, whose table was only about four feet away.

The henna job was watching them; she raised her large coffee in a toast.

Madonna?

"Like that, we might notice. But two ordinary women, not creating any problems..." He shook his head. "Sorry."

"It was later than this," said Martha. "The rush might have been over."

Mr. Vance shook his head again.

"Well, thank you," said Martha. "I apologize for bothering you."

"No problem." In seconds, Mr. Vance was back behind the new girl's shoulder.

Martha looked around for a vacant spot. Her gaze crossed Madonna's. The crone smiled, displaying impossibly white teeth, and waved her cup toward the vacant seat across from her.

One had been behaving crazily for some hours now; why not take up with a pro? Martha sidled past a cluster of loud-talking girls and took the vacant seat. "Thank you," she said.

The woman extended a hand, maneuvering dangling sleeves to avoid the debris on the tiny table. Her inch-long nails were crimson, the back of her hand was heavily veined and mottled with age spots, and the inner sides of her index and middle fingers were stained dark brown. "You may call me Madonna." Her voice was a smoker's rasp. "May I call you Martha?"

The woman had good hearing; Martha had spoken her name just once in introducing herself to Mr. Vance. "Of course." She shook Madonna's hand above the table. The bones felt like a loose bundle of twigs. "I'm happy to meet you, Madonna."

"I notice much," said Madonna.

"Indeed," said Martha. "You noticed my name."

"They"—the woman jerked her head toward the counter—"don't notice."

"They're very busy, of course."

"I notice. There are angels. And there are devils."

Martha sipped her coffee. It was tolerable. "So I understand."

"A balmy evening brings them out."

"Brings out angels and devils?"

One of the dough-and-glue objects that McDonald's calls an apple pie lay on its torn-open wrapper in front of Madonna. She set down her coffee cup, lifted the thing with both crimson-tipped hands, and took a dainty bite with those unreal teeth. She chewed elaborately. The column of her gullet convulsed in her wrinkled throat. She laid down the pie, took up a paper napkin, and dabbed her lips. The napkin came away crimson. "They didn't stay. It was balmy."

They. A specific *they?* Martha ventured a step into the maze. "Were they angels or devils?"

"Devils are angels."

"Ah. Just so." Was there sense in this Miltonic exercise?

Madonna took up her pie and nibbled. "Two," she said after another swallow. "As you said. Two. After that, one. Then one. A devil."

If there was sense…"Do you recall when this was?"

"Evening. But it was balmy."

"I see. Do you remember what day it was?"

"Moon-sabbath, as you said."

Moon-sabbath? As she had said?

She had asked Mr. Vance about customers on a Monday. Monday, moon-day—"A Monday?"

"In the common parlance, yes, Martha. Monday. Two moon-sabbaths past."

Two moon-sabbaths past—the Monday before last? The Monday that Wilma had been up here undergoing her psychiatric examination, getting her takeout, going home to her death.

"I see." Martha sipped her coffee.

Madonna said, "The fourth day of the solstice moon."

Madonna's use of *moon* was hard to follow. *Moon-sabbath* was Monday, all right, but *the solstice moon?*

Madonna nibbled at the apple pie.

Moon, to versifiers, meant *month.* The solstice moon might be the solstice month. The winter solstice occurred in December. "That would be December fourth? In the common parlance?"

Madonna smiled.

Martha edged ahead. "Could you describe them?" But of course, she had already described Enid and Wilma in Madonna's hearing; Madonna had only to repeat in her own curious idiom what Martha had said to Mr. Vance.

Madonna said, "The light one made itself dark, and the dark one made itself light."

Martha sipped coffee. *The light one*—Wilma Oberfell, perhaps, with her gray-blond hair and fair complexion. *Made herself dark?* Makeup? More likely clothing. Wilma had been wearing her good black coat, Tessie had said.

And Enid, *the dark one* with her olive skin and dark hair? At the office that Monday afternoon, she had been wearing something neutrally professional. She might have changed before going to the psychiatrist's office. "In the common parlance," ventured Martha, "do you mean the blond one was wearing dark clothes and the brunette one was wearing light clothes?"

"Light and heavy." Madonna's laugh was a hoarse cackle. "Heavy cream is light. It rises to the top." She set down the remains of the apple pie and carefully licked the fingers of her right hand. "They didn't stay."

One could ask Enid if she had been wearing a light-colored jacket that night, or perhaps a sweater or sweatshirt. Light-colored and heavy. Wilma, too, was light—fair—and heavy.

These word games were contagious.

But did any of this matter? One already knew that Enid and Wilma had stopped at a McDonald's. *They didn't stay.* Madonna might be confirming Wilma's takeout, if any confirmation was needed.

"The devil," said Madonna, "made itself black."

Martha ventured another inch. "Was there anything else about the devil?"

Madonna nibbled once more at the pie. She had consumed no more than a quarter of it; no doubt she had learned to extend her consumption over much of the evening. She patted at her lips again. "They eat and drink."

"I see."

"You see; I see."

"I see that you are a seer," said Martha.

Madonna cackled, her dentures bared to the artificial gums. "I don't always sit here."

"Where were you sitting, then?"

"A seer." She cackled again and looked off to one side. "Through the looking glass."

Looking glass? The place had no mirrored walls. Martha followed the direction of Madonna's gaze. The front windows reflected back the crowded interior. Aha. A window was glass; one looked through a window. Looking glass. "You saw them through—," and Martha nodded toward the windows.

Madonna cackled. "It was balmy. They sat." Like Martha, she nodded toward the windows. "They parted. The devil came around the corner."

"The devil?" Was there *any* sense in this?

"The devil." Madonna's eyes began wandering:

over to the windows, around the chattering crowds, up to the serving counter.

"Someone else?"

"Followed that one." Madonna seemed to have shrunk inside her layers; her gaze traveled everywhere but Martha's face.

"Are you all right?" asked Martha.

But she might have ceased to exist.

Her bony hands trembling, Madonna folded the wrapper around what remained of her pie, clutched her coffee cup, rose to her feet, and shuffled between tables to a vacancy across the room.

Martha didn't try to follow her. She finished off her cold coffee, dropped the cup into a trash can, and went out onto Broadway.

There were benches at the end of the median parkway; had Enid and Wilma sat there to talk? What had they talked about?

Who—what—was the devil who had come around the corner? Why did Madonna think he—it—had followed *that one?* Which one was *that one?*

One assumed it was Wilma, the victim.

What about that devil?

THE ANSWERING MACHINE was blinking when Martha arrived home. Francis McInerny's voice told her he was about to go into a meeting; he'd call back.

It was after nine when he called. His voice was steadier than it had been last week; he sounded ready to sell her underwater acreage in Florida.

"There's something I need to discuss with you," she said. "I'm going to be at your building tomorrow morning. Will you be in?"

"Unfortunately," he said, "I will not. But I have a moment or two just now."

The day had caught up with Martha. She said, "This must be discussed face-to-face."

"A serious matter, is it, then?"

"Have you heard that Howard Wallace was killed?"

"Killed? Holy saints." She envisioned a rapid sign of the cross. "And didn't I see him, alive and well, only last night at the board meeting? How was the man killed?"

"He was shot to death at the West Brooklyn office sometime during the night."

"God bless my soul." He fell silent for a moment. She heard voices and laughter in the background. "And what would you be wanting to talk with me about?" he asked. "For it was off and home I was as soon as the meeting was over. Left with two or three others and kept them company all the way to the Court Street station. There's a bar on the way, you know, the Rose of Sharon, where I passed many an hour in the bad old days, and it's easier to stay on the far side of the street if I'm well companied, if you take my meaning."

"Just so. I'm calling because we need to discuss some very odd information I have received. I shall have to give it to the police, but I've decided I must acquaint you with it first."

"Ah." Another silence. "Shall we, as they say, do lunch?"

Tessie Doone's Fairhearing should be finished by noon. "So long as I can get to Brooklyn Family Court by two o'clock."

It could be arranged. They settled on a coffee shop near Foley Square.

At ten o'clock Martha turned on the local news channel. At ten-oh-eight the anchor told her that the director of a Brooklyn Legal Aid office had been shot to death in his office. There followed a long shot of the office building that housed West Brooklyn Legal Services; a jiggly view of a Howard-length bundle being hustled into an ambulance; a close-up of Luther Young talking of the great loss to the poor people of our city. The next segment, sounding of sleigh bells, showed ice skaters in front of the Rockefeller Plaza Christmas tree.

TWENTY-FOUR

HOWARD'S DEATH, accompanied by a ten-years-out-of-date photograph, made the front page of the *Times*.

West Brooklyn was back in business: clients waited; phones beeped; computer screens flickered. The light was on in the corner office.

John looked up and flagged her as she passed. He looked better this morning, but stress lines still etched the skin around his mouth. "The powers that make and break," he said, "have made Luther acting project director." As he spoke, the intercom tone beeped. He picked up. Martha heard a rumble. "Yes, she is," he said and held out the phone. "Luther."

The bass rumble of the acting director said, "Ms. Patterson, this is Luther Young. Will you come along to the director's office, please." There was no question mark at the end.

A second of silence passed; then she said, "Very well, Mr. Young," cradled the phone, and looked at John.

He rolled his chair back and stood up. "I tried, Martha."

THE IMPOSING OLD CHAIR in front of the desk was gone; its replacement was inadequate to Luther's long, lean body. Martha sat in the chair she had sat in a week and a half ago while Howard warned against the Mother Teresa syndrome. She avoided looking at the large damp spot on the carpet. John sat in the other chair, back straight, arms folded, lips closed in a straight thin line.

For the first time in her life, Martha was being fired.

"Please understand, I do appreciate your concern for our clients," said Luther. "But in my judgment, it is inappropriate for someone without union status to occupy a union position. I ask you to please prepare a departure memorandum. John, as we discussed, you will reassign the cases to your unit staff."

"Mr. Young," said Martha, "I have a home Fair Hearing scheduled for one of your rent-strike clients in less than an hour, and tomorrow I have an emergency Article 78 proceeding in Kings County Supreme. Defaulting on those would be malpractice."

"I told you, Luther," John said, "I don't have the staff right now to cover them."

A five-second silence. "All right," said Luther Young. "But no later than the weekend." After another moment, "Please."

"NO SEVERANCE PAY," said Martha when they were safely down the corridor. "Is that a grievable issue?"

A snort of laughter.

"I'm not sure I understand his thinking. Surely with the funding cuts, he should welcome volunteers."

"Well, it's a little baroque," John said. "If there's to be a massive use of pro bonos down the road, the union is going to have to agree to a structure. You're a maverick."

"I see," she said.

"Actually, I'm not so sure it isn't just the joy of power. You were Howard's idea. Merry Christmas."

THE RENT STRIKE had evidently borne some fruit. The stair rail had been reattached to the wall, the mailboxes were intact, and the smell had abated, along with much of the litter.

Tessie showed her to the dinette table. The television was muted and the rear of the apartment was silent. "Is Kareem here?" Martha asked.

"He got this girlfriend, he don spen a lot a time here no more. You need him for this Fairhearin?"

"Oh, no," said Martha. "I just wondered."

The doorbell buzzed. Tessie rolled to the door and admitted a middle-aged man carrying a briefcase and a tape recorder; the administrative law judge from the State of New York had arrived to conduct the Fair Hearing.

After half an hour of desultory conversation, nobody had appeared from the City Department of Social Services. The ALJ switched on his tape recorder, listened to Tessie's testimony, took copies of the documents, announced into the recorder that the City had made no appearance, and closed the hearing. He told Tessie she'd get a decision in the mail and offered Martha a ride back to West Brooklyn.

She declined, not without reluctance.

"I AIN NEVER use no money in that bank account. The good Lord know I could use some, but that wouldn be right."

"The SSI people may ask the bank who made those withdrawals," said Martha.

"I never know they kin do that." The television muttered. "It ain mine. Never was."

"I'm not saying it was yours. I'm just considering what the SSI judge would think if it happened that you took any of the money out."

Another pause. "Not for me. Ain my money in there."

"But, you see, if you signed your name to the withdrawal—"

"Ain no way else. It's jus for my cousin. My cousin Kevin, he ax me get some out for him."

"I see," said Martha. "Then you may have to tell the judge why it was that you, here in Brooklyn, withdrew money from a bank account in Philadelphia to give to your cousin, who was right there in Philadelphia where the bank was."

Tessie's gnarled hands gripped each other in her lap. "Evbody makin trouble," she said.

"Tessie, I'm not saying you aren't telling the truth. All I'm saying is, if you *did* tell the judge something that wasn't true and they found out, they could make a lot of trouble."

"Makin plenty right now," said Tessie.

"I know."

"They's things, you gotta have money."

"Just so."

"He be goin to college nex term. He gotta get him a education. Like he say, black man, nobody don want you to have nothin good happen. He be straight ev since he come back, but them p'lice jus go on makin trouble." Tessie's eyes were fixed on some point over Martha's head. "I surely do need that SSI money." Once more her hands knotted in her lap. "You my lawyer, right? You cain tell nobody nothin I say, right?"

"It's a little more complicated than that."

For just a moment Tessie's face relaxed in the direction of a smile. "I guess evthing be more complicated than you can say easy."

"For instance," said Martha, "if I knew a client was lying under oath, I couldn't go on representing the client. But I'd have to know, not just guess."

"I surely do need that SSI money."

"It seems to me," said Martha, "that you may be in what we call a catch-22. But that's just a guess."

"Kareem, he got that girlfriend, he goin to college, he ain goin on payin my rent much more."

"Well," said Martha, "let's go through this together. The bankbook shows that the account is closed, so even on paper you don't have that resource anymore."

"Ain got no others neither," said Tessie.

"They might ask where the money went when the account was closed."

"Didn none of it come to me."

"If it didn't get paid to you, and if it isn't in some other account with your name on it—"

Tessie laid a hand on her bosom. "Swear t'God, they ain no money in no bank nowhere got my name on it."

"—then they should reinstate your SSI as of the day the bank account was closed. But we'd have a problem about getting you the retroactive money."

"That the back money, them checks they didn send me? Listen, they jus send my checks again, they can keep that back money. Ain but two months. Jus they leave Kareem alone."

"I understand. But there's a problem with that, too."

"They cain do that? Just keep that back money they didn send me and send me my checks now?"

"They could do that, yes. But they might not send you the whole amount of your checks."

"Now why they want to do that?"

"Well, before they cut you off, you were getting SSI checks for about three years while your name was on that bank account. On paper, you got three years of SSI you weren't entitled to. If you didn't have a hearing and show that the money wasn't ever yours, they could hold some money out of your checks until they took back everything they paid you during those three years."

"Whee-oo." Tessie shook her head. "And none a my money in that bank ever. But if I go to court, they gon find out I took some out."

"They might not, but I wouldn't be doing my job if I didn't warn you that they might."

"An if I say I don use none a that money for me, then they say, 'Well, Tessie, what you go do with that money?' An if I say I give it to my cousin Kevin in Philadelphia, they say, 'Well, Tessie, why cain your cousin in Philadelphia get that money out for hisself?' That how it gonna go?"

"I don't know if it will. It's what we call the worst-case scenario."

Tessie sighed again. "Kareem, he jus hafta hep some with the rent. I surely don know what that girlfriend say."

There seemed no end to the complications. "That could be a problem. If the SSI learns that somebody is helping you out, they'll call it income and cut your check some more."

"Cut it *more?*"

"Cut it by the amount of help somebody gives you."

"You mean, first they don give you nuff to pay the rent, then they don let nobody hep you out? Whee-oo! They *like* havin people in the street?"

"I sometimes wonder."

"Seem like they ain no end. Las couple days, they let up hasslin him, now they back again, tryna make out like he go over to your office t'other night, you know that? Tryna make out like he break in an shoot that Mr. Walls."

"Have they arrested him?"

"Ain got nothin arrest him *for*. He be over to his girlfriend the whole night. He jus bout livin there these days. They tryna make out she be lyin, but she don give in to that none. An now this new detective, he talkin bout Wilma again. They got more reason be hasslin Frank McInerny steada Kareem. He come back, you know."

"So I've heard."

"I don know why they don bust him. He was up there, that night she get kill. Kareem see him. Roun bout midnight, Kareem gettin home, he say he see Frank McInerny goin up the stairs to Wilma's."

"Did Kareem tell the police that?"

"Not first off. First off, he don want to say he be here that time a night Wilma gettin kill. He get his girlfriend say he be with her all night, he jus come home in the mornin, time to get ready for work. They don believe what she say, they keep hasslin her, so then he tell them how he come home roun midnight an see Frank goin up the stairs. After that, they quit hasslin him a couple days. Now they act like they don believe the girlfriend bout Mr. Walls t'other night. But she don give in on that."

"They haven't arrested him."

"Nothin arrest him for. Nor that night Wilma get kill, neither. More'n Kareem out there that night."

"You mean Mr. McInerny?"

"More'n him."

Tessie could talk in a straight line if it suited her. "If you saw something suspicious, you should tell the police."

"They ain gon believe me." But Tessie was bursting with a need to confide. "You be my lawyer, what I say, you cain tell nobody, right? I ain tellin no lies to no judge. They's somebody went up there, fellah all in black. Got a hood on, pull down, jus bout cover his face."

"You didn't mention this before," said Martha.

"They ax me, did I see somebody go up *with* Wilma. They don ax nothin bout *before*."

"Tessie—"

"See, why I don say nothin, a while there, I'm scared it be Kareem, goin up the roof. They's a way over the roof, three buildins over, they useta be sellin crack. The p'lice clean that place out back las summer, but a minute there, I'm scared they come back, sellin crack again."

"You'd know if Kareem was using crack, wouldn't you, by the way he acted?"

Tessie shook her head vigorously. "Wasn I *think*. Jus I be *scared* for a little while. You know how you get. Kareem, even back before, when he be holdin up that store, he ain usin no drugs. He see what drugs do to his momma an daddy, he don have no part of it. Holdin up that store, he jus get too smart for hisself, thinkin he get rich offa somebody else's work. He do time, he see that ain no way to be a man. He be straight now. Wasn I *think* he be doin nothin bad. Jus, these days, you get scared is all."

"What was it you saw?"

"This fellow, maybe bout Kareem's size, all in black with a hood pull all roun his face, goin up the stairs easy on his feet, like he be sneakin up. So I spect they got that crack shop goin again, he headin for the roof. But evbody say they ain sellin over there no more, so soon's I get my head straight, I go thinkin what this fellow be sneakin up there for? I don know nobody live upstairs look like that.''

''What time was this?''

''Whatever time Wilma an Frank be goin on downstairs.''

''Did you ever see him again?''

Tessie shook her head. There was a silence. Tessie said, ''Didn *see* him.''

Martha looked at her.

''Wilma get upstairs, I hear somethin.''

Martha waited.

''I tole you, that p'licewoman here with you? I listen a little bit to Wilma an Frank goin at it, I don want Wilma know I hear all that. I don want her hear me shut my door, so I jus push it to. It still be open just that bit. She get up to the fourth floor, I hear like this sorta, like gym shoes squeakin? Soun like a basketball game up there for a minute. An then Wilma slam her door.''

Gym shoes squeaking? ''You haven't told the police any of this?''

Tessie shook her head. ''See, first thing, I think how I be scared it be Kareem. An I think, I tell the p'lice bout any a this, maybe they gon have the same confusion I do. Thinkin it be Kareem.''

''Well, it may be a risk, Tessie, but you do have an obligation to tell what you know.''

The near-smile again. ''P'lice hasslin all the time, you don think much bout obli*gat*ion.''

"I suppose not. But as your lawyer, *my* obligation is to advise you what *your* obligation is."

"An I do what I want with the advice, right?"

Martha looked at her watch. The car service was due any minute. "Tessie, the other day you said Wilma brought your mail up sometimes. Do you remember if she ever brought up one of the checks from the bank?"

"I don recollect. Wasn more'n two, three times Wilma bring up my mail. Generally it Vibelle, comin home from school. You think it was Wilma tole the SSI I was gettin them checks?"

"Well, no. They find out those things by running your Social Security number through a computer."

BUT, she thought as the hired car jounced over potholes, if Wilma had noticed that Tessie was getting checks from a bank in Philadelphia, might she have guessed where the money had come from? Might the hooded figure on the stairs have been Kareem after all, not looking for drugs, but looking to silence a blackmailer?

TWENTY-FIVE

TERRIBLE THING,'' said McInerny. ''Prime of his life. A great loss.'' His back was to the rear wall; behind Martha's bench a partition projected a couple of feet. The waiter having taken their orders, they were for the moment as private as one can be in a public space on the island of Manhattan.

Martha said, ''Have the police talked with you since he was killed?''

''Waiting for me last night when I returned from St. Honoria's. I thank you for having given me the news. I wouldn't have wanted to learn it from them. I was no help to them, for as I told you, I left the board meeting with several others and went straight home. Not that I can absolutely prove it was straight home I went, but at least this time I *know* what I did.'' He forced a smile. ''Do they think there's a connection with Wilma?''

She said, ''I have no idea.''

''The reason I ask, they seem to be giving a fair amount of attention to one of the tenants. Young fellow, out and about a good deal at night. It crossed my mind that they might be taking that mysterious figger on the fire escape a bit more seriously than I thought.''

''I believe there's a problem with the man on the fire escape,'' said Martha.

''The Big Mac and fries? I don't know that I'd call it a problem. Fond of McDonald's as she was, she wouldn't have waited until she got home to eat it.

She'd have been smelling the stuff and her mouth would have been watering. If she didn't eat it where she got it, she'd have eaten it on the subway.''

"The empty containers were found in the garbage can under her sink.''

McInerny shook his head. "Not possible.''

"That was my information.''

"Not possible. She was a fanatic about garbage. Everything went out as fast as she was done with it. She'd never have brought them in.''

"But they were there. So if you're right, she must have eaten at home. That means your man was on the fire escape too early to have murdered her.''

"Even so,'' he said, "it's a riddle. Eating at home, she'd have bundled them up and put them out as soon as she'd finished. If it had food remains on it—even the tiniest crumb—out it went.''

"Out where?''

"Into the incinerator closet.''

"What's the incinerator closet?''

"Ah. The place was built before the City outlawed the burning of garbage, making a mess of the streets instead of the air. There's a closet on each floor and a chute set into the back wall, to send your trash down to the incinerator. These days, you're supposed to put your bags in the closet and the super is supposed to pick them up from there. For most, the word is *supposed*, but my dear friend Wilma was scrupulous.''

The waiter appeared, clattered their plates onto the table, and left them once more islanded.

McInerny said, "But look here. Suppose she did eat it on the train and carry in the wrappings, not being able to find a trash basket that wasn't overflowing. When she got home, she'd have put the wrappings in a bag and carried it out to the closet, and it would be no trouble for somebody lurking in the fourth-floor lobby, or even just passing by, to seize her and push her back in while she had the door open. Thinking, you know, to pick up what might be lying around her place that could be turned to a bit of profit. And then put her bag of garbage in the can under her sink rather than venture out into the hall again. And then, out the window and down the fire escape."

"Would she have gone out into the hall in her night-gown?"

"Ah, well." He sighed. "At times she was given to behaving in a seductive manner. She was quite the party girl in her younger days, she'd have you know. In her heart, she was still nineteen."

But none of this was why they were there. Martha pushed her plate to one side and spread clean napkins in the middle of the table. She took one of the photo-copies from her handbag, unfolded the pages, and laid them out.

McInerny's face reddened.

"The postmark is December eighth," she said. "Four days after she died. Did you mail it?"

McInerny turned redder.

She said, "The original appears to have been steamed open. I'm sure you're aware that fingerprints can be lifted from paper."

"Well, then…" He cleared his throat. "Denial would be fruitless, wouldn't it?"

Martha said, "I can't withhold this from the police."

After a pause, he said, "She left them in my apart-ment."

"Them?"

"I beg your pardon?"

"You said 'them.' This isn't the only one?"

"Ah. There were two. This one and another addressed to himself."

"To Howard?" That flicker of déjà vu. "Did you read that one as well?"

McInerny shook his head. "Himself I knew; who Martha Patterson might be, I hadn't an idea in my head. When I returned that evening, there they sat, alone and unexplained. Unstamped, as well. The mood I was in, I was annoyed, supposing she'd be stopping by to retrieve them."

"She couldn't have addressed the one to me until after she followed me home," said Martha. "That was well past five o'clock."

"And you're wanting to know if she would have stopped off in my place before heading back up to the shrink's. And the answer is yes. Her own place being what you might call overfull of her past life, and mine being all but empty, she had taken to leaving her best clothes in my uncrowded closet, so as not to wrinkle them. Leaving something behind would give her a reason to come back, if she thought she needed one."

"I see. And did she ask for them when she came back?"

"In the event, no. Nor did I mention them. I was thinking only of how I might keep her out without undue discourtesy. I suppose I must have picked them up when I went upstairs to try to make amends. I was mystified when they turned up in my pocket in White Plains." He patted the breast of his jacket. "Not seeing any way of bartering them for a Metro-North ticket, I slipped them back and forgot them all over again. I didn't rediscover them until I was disposing myself to sleep at St. Honoria's. Not until then was I settled

enough to grow curious. From the shapes, it might be
that Wilma was wishing the two of you the joys of the
season. But not necessarily. She would save the odd
envelope when she'd use a card but not the envelope,
with a little gift, as it might be. Great one for little
gifts, she was—''

"You steamed it open," said Martha, "and found it
wasn't a Christmas card."

"It's not as straightforward as it sounds, steaming
open an envelope. And after all, I still had no idea who
Ms. Martha Patterson might be. It wasn't until later,
after meeting you and finishing with the police and
settling once more in my own apartment, that I thought
the best thing was to send them along to their intended
recipients."

"You just mailed them. Four days after you found
them in your apartment, you just dropped them in the
mail."

"First buying a pair of stamps. There's no way out
of it, is there? If fingerprints won't do the trick, my
DNA will turn up on the stamps."

"Why didn't you simply give them to the police?"

"My dear lady, you're supposing I was in my right
mind. I wanted no more to do with the police, but I
thought someone should know about them."

"You won't escape the police, however," she said.
"I'll be giving this to them as soon as possible. I'd
have done so yesterday, but I felt obliged to let you
know first." Martha began to gather up the photocop-
ies. "Wilma speaks of 'stealing from the system.' You
knew her well. What do you think she was talking
about?"

"Welfare, I should think."

All at once, for no reason she could identify, Martha's breath came short. "Why?"

"It's the first thing she'd think of. She worked for them once."

"For—?"

"The Department of Social Services. Department of Antisocial Disservices, she liked to call it. She hated it when she had to go into the system herself."

TWENTY-SIX

THE KNOT in Martha's stomach left no room for lunch; once more she left a BLT lying untouched.

When the IRT discharged her in front of the Kings County Courthouse with half an hour to spare, she went in at the end that housed Brooklyn Surrogate's Court, entered the file room, and called up the will of Anthony Collins.

It held no surprises. He had left all of which he had been possessed—a net estate, after taxes and the executor's fee, of $3,873.29—to his infant daughter, Rosemary Oberfell. What Martha was after was the name of the executor, and there it was: his attorney, Jerome Sternfield.

Martha had a passing acquaintance with Jerome Sternfield. She called from a telephone in the hall. He was in; if she was free in a couple of hours, he would be pleased to receive her.

She crossed the street to family court.

The Zables had brought Rosemary; for the first time, Martha had a look at the object of controversy. A sturdy little chunk with cherub cheeks and creamy blond curls, she sat stolidly on Neil Zable's lap, shielded from the rest of the courtroom by his broad shoulders.

Maurie Kimmel and Judge Harry Wallerstein had heard of Howard's murder, of course; their off-the-record curiosity was no less nerve-jangling for being masked as shock and sympathy. Once the case was

officially called, however, the formalities of the courtroom calmed her. She responded to Maurie Kimmel's
motion for dismissal with a simple, "No objection."
With a thump of the gavel, Judge Wallerstein said,
"Granted," putting to an end any claim Wilma Oberfell's ghost might have had on Wilma Oberfell's
daughter.

Martha turned from the counsel table in time to see
Neil Zable blink two or three times. He got to his feet
holding Rosemary as if he had dragged her from a
burning building.

Tears. Those were tears that Neil had been blinking
away.

Following him into the aisle, Geraldine exclaimed,
"Thank goodness," raised her fingers to her lips, and
said, "Oh, dear, I don't mean—"

Behind them, the gavel thumped and the judge said,
"Please."

Kimmel hustled them out the door, held out his
hand, said, "Martha, be well," and went off into the
stairwell.

Geraldine said, "Mrs. Patterson, could we have coffee or something?"

Astonished, Martha stalled by looking at her watch.

"Do you have time? I do so want to talk to somebody—you saw her..." Her voice trailed away.

There was plenty of time. And the Oberfell case was
closed; there remained no ethical prohibition against
talking with the adversary.

From her perch in Neil's arms, Rosemary declared,
"Santa Claus!"

"We're going," said Neil.

"Now."

"We're going. You coming or staying, Gerry?"

Geraldine was still looking at Martha.

Martha said, "I wouldn't like to hold up Rosemary's visit to Santa Claus."

"Oh, I can meet them afterward. She'll behave better with just him anyway."

Surprising Martha, Neil said, "Give her a chance to talk, Mrs. Patterson," and then rather spoiled the effect by adding, "Then maybe I can hear about something else."

Martha glanced at her watch once more, but it was purely a ritual gesture. "Very well," she said.

"THEY ALWAYS SAY one sister is the pretty one and one is the smart one. She was the pretty one. She was just beautiful. That means I should have been the smart one, but she got straight A's. It seemed like there was always one subject I got a B in." Stirring her coffee around and around, Geraldine said, "I don't know how she did it. From the time she was a baby, she was just impossible to control. I'm five years older, but I was still living at home when she was in high school, so I had to hear all about it. She was the smart one *and* the pretty one. But I was the good one and she was the bad one."

Martha's appetite had crept back. She tried to chew her replacement BLT quietly.

"And she could sing like an angel. In church, in the choir, she was always the soloist. She sang 'The Impossible Dream' at graduation."

"I suppose," said Martha, "Rosemary looks a good deal as Wilma did at that age."

"Oh, any three-year-old is cute, but Wilma was beautiful. I was so glad she named the baby Rosemary. Our parents gave us such ugly names."

There was no adequate response; Martha attempted none.

"But it just never came to anything. She started to Brooklyn College, but she got married her freshman year and dropped out and moved to California. Mother and Daddy didn't like him. I didn't like him either. I don't even think Wilma liked him. I thought maybe he got her pregnant, but—well, I don't know, but they didn't have a baby. And then that broke up and she came back. She got married again, and that one didn't work out either. That one didn't want children, and he used to hit her. She started to"—Geraldine's voice dropped a tone—"drink a lot, and... Well, I shouldn't talk, but I haven't put on anything like the weight she did. Of course, she was a big-boned girl; we're both big-boned. Anyway, they got divorced too."

"Did you know Rosemary's father?"

"Oh, Tony was nice. He came to see the baby a lot before he got too sick. He was good for Wilma. She took off a lot of that weight when she started seeing him. But that didn't work out, either."

"He was ill, of course."

"I thought it was only children who got leukemia, but grown-ups can get it too. He got sick before his divorce came through, and he wouldn't get married again. He said he wasn't going to saddle Wilma with a sick man, but I just know there was more to it than that. He cared a lot about Rosemary, but I think he just didn't want to marry Wilma. I thought she got pregnant so he'd marry her, but he didn't."

"I see."

"She was thirty-seven. I don't care what they say; I think that's just too old to get pregnant. And then Tony didn't marry her, and she got so depressed. I talked to the social worker, and they didn't let her take the baby home from the hospital, and then she was in and out of the mental ward for almost a year after the baby was born. They put her on medical leave from her job, and then finally they just terminated her.''

"It's lucky for Rosemary that you were willing to take her.''

"Oh, I was glad to. Kim and Brad—my children?— they were getting so big; Kimberley was seventeen at the time and Bradley was twelve. I was thrilled to have a baby in the house again.''

"How did they feel about it? And your husband?''

"Oh, the children just adored her. She was like their little doll. And Neil—it was so wonderful. He never liked Wilma—he always thought she was a bad influence on the children, and he was really disgusted when she got pregnant—but he just fell in love with the baby. And she just adores him. You know how it is; I'm the one that has to say no all day, and then he comes home and plays with her.''

So much for first impressions. Martha said, "I heard a rumor that Rosemary was supposed to get a lot of money from her father.''

"I don't know what would give anybody such an idea. Tony's medical bills just ate everything up. It wasn't even four thousand dollars is all he had left, and the lawyer's keeping that in a special account until all this—well, I guess it is over with, isn't it? We're going to invest it for Rosemary so she'll have a little bit started for college, anyway. It just gets more and more expensive, and with the economy the way it is, you know. And the only money Wilma left was her little bit of a Social Security death benefit, and that doesn't even cover the funeral.''

"You said Wilma was working before she got pregnant."

"For the welfare department." Geraldine sighed. "With her brains, you'd think she could have had any kind of exciting job she wanted, but she ended up working for the welfare department. She really hated it. I think that's one of the reasons she got so depressed. And that terrible place she moved into, with all the blacks and drugs. And that man McInerny. An alcoholic himself." Geraldine set down her coffee cup, reached up, and fished a tissue out of the pocket of the coat she had hung at the end of the booth. She wiped her eyes and blew her nose. "I'm sorry. I just feel so bad. I should have had her living with me."

"Surely that would have been a considerable disruption."

"But she was my little sister. Oh, Mrs. Patterson, can you believe, I even tried to help her fix up that apartment? It was a good neighborhood once, before all the blacks and Puerto Ricans moved in. That man McInerny lived there for years before it tipped—you know what I mean—and I guess he was just too drunk to ever move out. So I told myself—like I was lying to myself, you know—I pretended it was really OK; there was still a white man living there. I told her, 'I'll come over and help you sort through those boxes, get rid of all that old stuff you aren't using, make yourself a real home.' But she was so funny about throwing things out. She kept saying it was still good stuff. She was saving old clothes from when she still had her figure and things from when she lived in a bigger place. I said, 'Well, if it's good enough for somebody to use, we'll bring it out to my place and have a tag sale.' But she just wouldn't. I said, 'It's no wonder you have mice and roaches, with all that stuff sitting around.' I just couldn't believe it when she wanted to take Rosemary back to live in that awful place.''

''Why did she suddenly decide she wanted Rosemary?''

''She said Tony dying made her think how she didn't have anybody of her own.'' She wiped her eyes again. ''I just couldn't understand her at all. She had all that stuff sitting around, but at the same time she was just fanatical about garbage. She wouldn't leave any garbage in the kitchen. Not even in the garbage can. As soon as she was finished with a meal, out everything would go, even just a dry cereal box. She used up plastic bags like—'' Geraldine wiped her eyes again. ''I don't know why I'm going on like this, about garbage.''

''Always? She always threw out her garbage?''

''Every single time.''

''Did you by any chance tell that to the police?''

''The police?''

''They found McDonald's containers in her garbage can,'' said Martha. ''Under her sink.''

''McDonald's?''

''The hamburger place.''

''No, I know what you mean. She liked McDonald's. I'm just so surprised. They'd been used? I mean, they were greasy?''

Martha said, ''We know she stopped in a McDonald's for takeout after her psychiatric examination. Her lawyer was with her, and somebody else in the McDonald's remembers seeing them. And the wrappers were in her garbage can under the sink when she was found the next morning.''

''My goodness.''

"So naturally I'm wondering if you told the police about her habit of taking her garbage out right away."

Geraldine shook her head. "It never came up."

"She was in her nightgown when I found her," Martha said. "Her bed was unmade. It appeared that she ate her takeout and threw the wrappers into the garbage can, undressed and was watching Channel 13 in bed, and was surprised by an intruder, who possibly came in the fire escape window."

"But—" Geraldine broke off and, after a moment, shook her head.

Martha said, "Just so."

"It sounds like somebody oh, my goodness. Like somebody was trying to make it look like she went to bed after she ate, only they didn't know she had that thing about garbage."

"That's assuming she absolutely *never* went to bed without taking the garbage out."

"She was the same way at my place."

"It's a piece of information the police should have."

"Oh, dear," said Geraldine.

"Do you have the precinct telephone number?"

"Oh, that woman." Geraldine folded her hands on the table. "I really can't bring myself to talk to that woman."

"Detective Jamison?"

"I guess that's her name. That skinny woman with the funny hair. She looks like a half-breed, like she's Indian and Negro mixed or something. She wanted *alibis*. Like we were *murderers*. My own *sister*."

Martha said, "I don't think you should take it personally. They wanted my alibi, too."

But Geraldine was not to be pacified. "She acted like she had to know where he was every *minute* that night, and then that other one, the Italian one, he started in. It wasn't enough Neil was at the Queens store filling in for the night manager. They just don't let you have any *privacy*."

Neil was not in custody. Martha said, "I assume he was able to satisfy them about being at the store."

"Oh, he satisfied them all right. He had an *alibi*, all right." Geraldine's voice cracked. "It's so tacky. I wish they'd left us alone. I wish I'd never found out." Tears trickled over her lower lids. "The night cashier. He was you know, with the night cashier. Out in the parking lot, in the backseat, like high school kids. Everybody on the night shift *knew*. It's so *tacky*."

TWENTY-SEVEN

So what's your interest in Tony Collins's estate?" said Jerome Sternfield. "I heard you retired."

He would surely have heard about Howard; she couldn't face the commotion that would result from telling the full story. "I've been doing a little pro bono work," she said.

"Can't stay out of harness?"

"Well, it's not for the long term, but it involved me in representing the mother of his child."

"The recently deceased mother."

"Just so." Her conversation with Geraldine had blunted the point of this visit, but she was here, and so she said, "I've been wondering what the child's expectations might be."

"From Tony? Three thousand and change. It's in escrow pending resolution of the custody suit."

"As of about an hour ago, the custody suit is resolved."

"Good. It's loose change these days, but she might as well have it. Tony was a hell of a nice guy with decent earning capacity, but his assets were down the tube. The man was sick for years, and his medical insurer shafted him early on."

Jerome Sternfield's fees were not those of a mass-production legal clinic. She said, "But he retained you for a will he could have made with a kit from a stationery store."

"Oh, well, that was my little bit of pro bono. I'm

on retainer to the ex-wife's family. I drew up Tony's original will while he was still one of them and I liked the guy, so I did the new one gratis after the kid was born.'' He responded to her unuttered question: "No conflict of interest. The marriage was childless, and the ex-wife formally relinquished all interest in Tony's miserable estate. Trust me, she doesn't need it."

"Could there possibly be other assets? Perhaps something on the order of a life estate in Tony Collins, remainder to go to Rosemary?"

"What a lovely dream. Could there be? We never say never, so sure, there *could* be. And Sasquatch and the Loch Ness monster could be cruising in the Bermuda Triangle. Watch out if that pregnancy comes full-term."

"No hidden inheritance."

"The only money belongs to the ex-wife's family, and there's no way they'd set up anything in favor of Tony's little bastard. When Tony left their darling daughter's house and home he became a nonperson, and the kid doesn't exist."

"I see."

"So what's your interest, now that your client's out of the picture?"

"I suppose—" She broke off. She had intended to make a facetious reference to Wilma's ghost, but once more her thought processes seemed scrambled. Commanding herself to remain coherent, she said, "None, really. It's just that no guardian *ad litem* was appointed for the child and I felt I should have a look before closing the case." She got to her feet. "I really shouldn't be taking up your time."

"A pleasure." As he stood, his face sobered. "I'm

sorry. Your husband passed away recently, didn't he? My condolences.''

"Thank you," she said.

He walked her to the elevator; as she stepped in, he said, "Take it easy, Martha."

A NORTH WIND gusted against her back, spiraling paper scraps and grit high into the air.

Take it easy.

It was not just a routine phrase of farewell; she had detected concern in Jerome Sternfield's voice. She feared she was making a spectacle of herself.

The Zables were out of it. There was no secret inheritance, and even though Neil Zable clearly felt Rosemary had escaped from something akin to a burning building, he was not under arrest and his embarrassing alibi rang true. And then there was Olivia Ullbright's question: How could the expectation of money from Tony Collins's estate possibly give rise to the language of Wilma's letter?

Martha had been obsessed—the word was not too strong—obsessed with that notion of a secret inheritance.

Obsessions, of course, are the mind's masks for realities too disturbing to be faced. Back among hidden synapses, some unpleasant awareness must be struggling to break into her consciousness, while her mind struggled with equal vigor to force it back into the depths. Thus these lapses into mental muddle.

Take it easy.

Just so. There was no mediating these internal disputes on the conscious level. The forces of the unconscious must fight it out, as it were, offstage. One could do no more than tend conscientiously to the mundane.

She considered the mundane. She had to write her departure memo. Tomorrow she would hold a final case conference with John, and then she would be free—

Free?

She had believed she didn't want to leave West Brooklyn; Luther's determination to dispense with her services had outraged her. But all at once she was eager to be quit of the place. She would finish her departure memo and hand off her cases to John first thing in the morning, and before lunch she'd march out the door into the rest of her life. She had no very clear idea what the rest of her life might entail, but it was out there somewhere. Would her knees, she wondered, accommodate cross-country skiing?

She pushed through into the welcome absence of wind and rode to the fourth floor. It was surprising how familiar had become the mud-colored waiting-room carpet, the shabby clients waiting on the cheap chairs, the faint smell of sweat, Gloria-the-receptionist's nod of greeting. The nod was sober-faced today.

Eager was the wrong word. There would be a loss. No wonder she felt muddled.

Anita Pagan's door opened as Martha approached, and a man stepped into the corridor. She recognized him; it was the detective who had questioned her after Howard's murder. She even recalled his name. He was thin and bony and quick-moving; he was sharp-angled; his name was Sharpman. He was carrying a zip-top satchel in one hand.

Anita's eyes had followed Sharpman into the corridor. Her elfin face was drawn; she acknowledged Martha, barely, with a little nod. Martha forced down another surge of anxiety and said, "Good afternoon, Mr. Sharpman."

He said, "Hello, Ms. Patterson." Detectives couldn't allow themselves lapses about names.

It occurred to her that his presence could be counted a boon, for she must give Wilma's letter to the police without further delay. She had meant to call Detective Jamison, but Sharpman was on the spot. She said, "Could I speak to you for a moment?"

"Sure," he said. No detective, she realized, would turn down such a request from a witness.

He took the client chair and said, "Tell you what. As long as I'm here—" He set the satchel on his lap, unzipped it, and pulled out a black bundle in a plastic bag. He slid the bundle from the bag and leaned forward to spread it on Martha's desk. "I wonder if you recognize this. You can handle it. Forensics is finished with it."

It was a grubby black sweatshirt. She pulled it to lie straight. It was faded, frayed at the cuffs, streaked with dried mud. It had a hood. He had just been talking with Anita.

She said, "I can't say positively that I recognize it, but I did see a sweatshirt much like it the first day I was in this office. It was cold and Anita Pagan was wearing it to keep warm. Does she recognize it?"

"What day was that?"

"A week ago Monday."

"Do you remember if you saw it anytime after that?"

That unpleasant tremor started up again in her midsection. "When I left the office that evening, it was hanging on a hook beside the door to the waiting room. I noticed it because I took my coat from the hook next to it."

"What time was that?"

"About a quarter after five, I suppose." She added, "Anita had left."

He smiled. "Was anybody else still here?"

"Oh, yes. Lights were still on in several offices, and there were two clients in the waiting room talking with a Landlord-Tenant lawyer—I believe her name is Deborah Schwartz—and with Carlos Quinones, who was a paralegal in the Landlord-Tenant Unit." Sharpman had taken out a notebook. "Then Enid Morgan came off the elevator. And John Ainsworth was there. He left with me. That's all I can recall."

"Was it there the next day?"

"I don't know. I didn't hang my coat there after the first day."

"Did you ever see it again?"

"Not that I recall. Oh. If this is any help, it wasn't there the following Monday." Sharpman looked up and she said, "It was cold in the office again. It generally is on Mondays. But that morning, Anita wasn't wearing it and I remember looking around a bit. The cardigan she had on was so ugly, I wondered why she was wearing it instead of the sweatshirt. I recall looking on the hook by the door and discovering that it wasn't there. After that, it went out of my mind."

"Do you know who it belonged to?"

"I have no idea."

"OK." He shut his pen inside his notebook and laid it on her desk, stuffed the sweatshirt back into the plastic bag, and tucked it into the satchel. "Now, there was something you wanted to see me about."

She unzipped the center compartment of her handbag and took out the tissue-wrapped letter from Wilma Oberfell. "I found this in my mail Tuesday evening when I got home from work." She laid it on the desk and rolled her chair back to enable Sharpman to hitch his chair closer.

He slid the pen out of the notebook and pushed the tissue back with the blunt end until he could read the face of the envelope. Making use of the tissues, he eased the letter out and unfolded it. When he finished reading, he examined the envelope. "Do you know her handwriting?"

"I'm no expert, but it looks like her signature on some documents in the file."

"It looks as if it was opened and resealed. Mailed December eighth. Do you know how it got into the mail?"

"As a matter of fact, I do. Francis McInerny—" She looked a question; Sharpman nodded. "Mr. McInerny says he found it in his apartment that Monday and mailed it Friday."

"You've discussed it with him?"

"He's a client. I felt an ethical obligation." Sharpman's face sharpened, and she sensed that unspoken, *Lawyers!* "I got it the night before Howard...before Howard was killed. I'd meant to pass the buck to him."

"But he wasn't in any condition to accept the buck."

"Just so. And since I believed Mr. McInerny was the likeliest person to have put it in the mail, I had an obligation to let him know I was going to pass it along to the police."

"Have you told anybody else?"

"No. I must tell you that he said he found another letter with it, addressed to Howard Wallace."

"What happened to that one?"

"He said he mailed it as well."

"Anybody see it?"

"I don't know. I assume if it had been in his office, your people would have found it."

"Wasn't in his apartment, either." Sharpman tapped his pen beside the letter. "This sounds like more of what she was saying to you the day she was killed." Using the tissue, he turned pages. " 'There is stealing going on.' Funny way to put it. Not 'So-and-so is stealing.' "

"I wish I'd listened to her."

"You couldn't know her head was on straight. The judge did order a psychiatric examination."

"It's common in custody battles. It doesn't at all imply that she was given to paranoid fantasies."

"OK, and somebody thought it was worthwhile strangling her, so it's possible she did have something on somebody. What do you think she meant by *stealing from the system?*"

"It seems she was a welfare caseworker at one time."

"People on the inside. Blowing the whistle. Covering up. She thought somebody in the office was involved."

It wasn't quite a question; Martha didn't answer.

"Quinones?" Sharpman seemed to be thinking out loud. "But what system would he have been stealing from?"

Martha said nothing.

"Doesn't this office handle welfare cases?"

"It's this unit that handles them, in fact," she said. "Mr. Sharpman, what is the significance of the sweatshirt?"

She expected an evasion, but he said, "Forensics found black fibers embedded in Wilma Oberfell's neck and on her nightgown. Cotton and acrylic, most likely from a cheap sweatshirt. This one turned up in a vacant lot a couple of blocks from her building. The fibers are a match.''

''You think somebody from the office wore it during the attack and then threw it away?''

''It's a reach, but they've run out of leads at her building. Nobody don' know nothin'.''

''Kareem Hewitt is out of it?''

A sharp glance.

''His grandmother is my client. She complained that he'd been hassled.''

''Considering the tall tales he tried, he's lucky it was only hassle.''

''But he's in the clear?''

''When somebody did Wilma Oberfell, he was shooting baskets in a school yard. He was afraid we'd find out they were smoking a little pot.'' He tapped his pen beside the letter again. ''It's nice you got around to producing this. I'll give you a receipt.'' He took a pad from a jacket pocket. As he scribbled, he said, ''Do you know anybody who wears a wig?''

''A wig?''

Pen in hand, he gestured over the top of his head. ''Black wig, Negroid type.''

''Not that I'm aware of. Why?''

''Forensics found a hair inside the hood from a natural-hair Afro wig.'' He tore off the receipt and laid it on the desk.

She said, ''I assume you know that Mr. McInerny saw somebody on the fire escape wearing something black with a hood.''

''Yes.''

''Isn't there a problem involving McDonald's take-out?''

"Who's been talking?"

"I believe someone told Enid Morgan. The reason I ask—Mr. McInerny and Geraldine Zable, independently, have told me that Wilma wouldn't have left food containers in her garbage. She was obsessive about getting garbage out of the apartment."

He took up his notebook and pen again.

"Something else," she said. "I came across a strange woman, who calls herself Madonna, at a McDonald's near the Seventy-second Street IRT station. She speaks in riddles, but I believe she saw Wilma and Enid getting the takeout on the night in question. It's just a few blocks from the psychiatrist's office."

"Madonna?"

Martha described her.

He made another note, looked up, and said, "Have you got any more surprises for me?"

"Not that I can think of."

Once more he folded his pen into his notebook. He took a plastic bag from the satchel, slid the tissue-wrapped letter into it, and tucked the whole thing away. He took a business card from a pocket and laid it on her desk. "In case something else comes up," he said, "how about getting to me a little faster? There is a little thing you may have heard of called withholding evidence."

TWENTY-EIGHT

MARTHA CLOSED HER DOOR behind Detective Sharpman and made herself inhale deeply and exhale forcefully.

Work. The mundane. The departure memo.

She took a handful of folders from her file, pulled a yellow legal pad in front of her, and picked up her pen.

TO: John

That annoying tremor was affecting her penmanship. The *h* in John's name had gone awry; her hand had separated the little hump after the loop and made it into a little loop by itself. What she had written looked more like *Jolen* than *John*. She laid down the pen and shook her right hand.

Jolen.

Her mind added another little loop and the name sprang from its hiding place in the back of her mind.

Jolene.

Howard, standing in front of the open file drawer, darkness outside the window: "Do you know anything about an Armbruster case? Jolene Armbruster?"

Jolene Armbruster. She wrote it on the yellow pad so that it should not escape her again.

It was like the toppling of the first domino.

Wilma had written two letters, and here was the explanation of that nagging déjà vu. Martha had seen the one addressed to Howard. It had been in the bundle of mail she had dealt out the other morning, a greeting-card envelope with a handwritten address, and she had placed it in Howard's box. She even remembered the round looping handwriting.

What morning was that?

She had just returned from court. She had stopped at the mailboxes to chat with John. He had gone off to answer his phone, and she had taken up the bundle of mail.

She reached for her desk calendar. It was Monday morning that she had been in court on the emergency eviction case. It was that same Monday, said her calendar, that Kareem had brought in the Kevin Hill affidavit. So it was that same night, Monday night, that she had discovered the theft of her billfold and had returned to the office, to find Howard searching the Government Benefits Unit's files for a Jolene Armbruster case.

Had Wilma's letter to Howard named a name? Jolene Armbruster? "You should look at a Jolene Armbruster case" perhaps?

Another domino toppled: She had told Sharpman that John had left with her on that first Monday, while the sweatshirt was still hanging harmlessly on the hook by the door. But he hadn't. John had ridden down in the elevator with her, but he hadn't left the building with her. He had gone back up, saying he had forgotten something.

For several minutes Martha sat motionless. Then she pushed back her chair, opened her office door, and started up to the front.

As she passed Anita's office, Anita looked up and beckoned her in. Her pixie face was still anxious. "What did he want?" she said.

"The sweatshirt," said Martha. "If I'd seen it after that Monday when you had it on."

"I hung it out by the door where it always was, and that's the last I saw it."

"Just so. I saw it there when I left, and never again. Whose is it?"

"It's just the office sweatshirt. I always tried to grab it on Mondays because it's comfortable. Then it disappeared and I was stuck with that awful cardigan."

"Do you think the one he had was it?"

"It has the same label, half torn out like that one."

Martha said, "Oh, dear."

Anita said, "No."

"No what?"

"Not Carlos. Carlos wouldn't kill anybody. He *couldn't*."

"Anita—"

"It's just crazy to think he could. Anyway, he was driving. He drives for a car service when he needs money. Six o'clock to midnight. Even if they thought he could possibly kill somebody, the times—"

"Anita."

Anita stopped.

"Howard said Carlos might engage in larceny but not murder. That's good enough for me." The thudding of her heart was almost painful. "Do you know if Detective Sharpman has left?"

"What do you want with him?"

Tell her about Jolene Armbruster? Martha hesitated, then drew back. "Just something I forgot to mention. Nothing to do with Carlos. I'd better see if he's still here."

But Gloria-the-receptionist said Detective Sharpman had left a few minutes ago.

Martha found his business card on her desk. The precinct said he was gone for the day. She left her numbers, office and home.

Then she sat for some minutes looking at "Jolene Armbruster" on her yellow pad. Then she reached across her desk for the Brooklyn telephone directory.

WELFARE ADVOCATES Organization was a twenty-five-minute bus ride away, on the upper floor of a two-story commercial building in a working-class neighborhood. A small sign halfway down a side street marked the entrance. Martha was immediately buzzed in and found Sunny Searle waiting in an open door at the top of a flight of concrete stairs. Stepping into an overheated space as large as half a gymnasium, Martha said, "It's very good of you to see me." No one else seemed to be around.

"No problem." Sunny bolted the door behind her. "The Job Club isn't until six-thirty." She hung Martha's coat on a rack. "Would you like some coffee?"

She wouldn't really, but it would serve as a breather before the plunge. "Yes, I think I would. Thank you."

So they executed the coffee and sugar and milk routine, and then Sunny led Martha around a long conference table, a collection of mismatched chairs, and a free-standing blackboard, into a five-by-seven area enclosed by head-high partitions. Sunny sidled around a desk that filled half the space and waved Martha into an armchair jammed into the remaining corner.

Martha took a sip of her coffee. It had been reheated too often; its bitterness threatened to gag her. "I'm afraid I sounded quite addled on the phone," she said.

"Everybody's upset," said Sunny.

"Just so. I'm here because something has happened

that I don't understand, and I hoped you might be able to help." Martha set her mug on the corner of Sunny's desk and opened her handbag. "This is a photocopy of something I found in my mail Tuesday night. I'd appreciate your telling me what it suggests to you." She passed the copy of Wilma's letter across the desk. "If anything."

Sunny leafed through to the last page, looked at Martha, then turned back and began to read. For several minutes there was no sound but the rustling of the pages. When she finished the last page, she said, "Is this genuine?"

"I believe so."

"Why are you showing it to me?"

Martha said, "It implies that somebody in West Brooklyn Legal Services is perpetrating a fraud on some 'system.' At the Christmas party, Anita mentioned a conference your organization put on a few years ago, at which a welfare official talked about a way of defrauding the welfare system. And two of the people who attended that conference are now working at West Brooklyn."

Sunny said nothing.

"Anita, who is the one who brought up the subject," Martha said, "and"—she tried not to emphasize his name—"John."

Still Sunny said nothing.

Martha said, "Could you tell me how the subject came up?"

After another moment of silence, Sunny seemed to reach a decision. "It wasn't any big thing," she said. "A bunch of us went out for a drink after the last session. This AOM was on the edge of drunk, and John was doing his charm thing. You know how he does—he can't help it; it's just the way he comes on.''

''Just so.''

''They were kidding around, sort of carrying on the role-playing, pushing it into outrageous scenarios.''

''Did she say how the scheme would work?''

''Yes, but anybody who knows how the system works could figure it out. Somebody on the inside creates fictional cases on the computer and forges the paper files, and somebody on the outside picks up the grants.''

''Why would one need an outside confederate? It would mean splitting the money.''

''She'd need somebody to sit for the photo ID. She wouldn't want to risk it herself. And she'd have to be running several cases to make it worth the effort, so she sure couldn't sit for the photographer over and over. And then she couldn't use an ID to pick up the grant with somebody else's picture on it.''

''Would it be worth the risk for the outside people? A welfare grant is very small potatoes.''

''There wouldn't be that much risk. Picking up the grant, you're at the window for five minutes, max. If the grant is in the computer, nobody really looks at you. And you'd create cases with a lot of children. Maybe several for each runner.''

Martha said, ''A case with, say, five children—''

Sunny had it memorized: ''With the maximum rent allowance, 442 semimonthly.''

''Eight hundred eighty-four dollars a month for each case. It would have to be split with the inside person, but it would be tax-free.''

''And food stamps,'' said Sunny.

Martha said, "Do you remember that woman's name?"

Sunny shook her head. "It was three years ago."

"Do you have an attendance record?"

"I doubt it. The files from back then are chaos. I could look, but it could take a year to find anything."

"When people performed the role-plays," said Martha, "did they use their own names or fictional names?"

"Fictional."

"Were the names assigned or did they pick their own?"

"Just the roles were assigned. They picked names for themselves. What are you after?"

Martha hesitated, doubtful about the wisdom of her next question. But there was something trustworthy about Sunny Searle. "Have you ever heard the name Jolene Armbruster?"

After a moment's thought, Sunny said, "I don't think so. Not that I can remember. Who's Jolene Armbruster?"

"That's what I'd like to find out. Howard said he'd had an inquiry about a Jolene Armbruster case and he thought it might be one of our clients. But there wasn't any case under that name in the computer. I wondered if it meant anything to you."

"Not that I can remember. Is it important?"

"I think it could be. I have reason to think Howard also received a letter from Wilma, on Monday. Monday night he was looking for a Jolene Armbruster case, and Tuesday night he was killed. It wasn't until today that I remembered." She drew in a breath. "And then I noticed the initials." Sunny frowned, and Martha said, "J.A."

"I know what you mean. I'm just trying to follow your logic." Sunny's voice had taken on an edge.

"I'm not sure *logic* is the word. Frightful things have been happening, and I'm looking for connections."

"Logic, connections, whatever. I think what you're saying is that three years ago, in a bar, a drunken welfare official talked to five or six people about how to defraud the welfare system. One of them was John Ainsworth. Three years later, Wilma Oberfell writes you a letter saying somebody is stealing from the system. She doesn't say what system, and she names no names. OK so far?"

"Add the fact that Wilma Oberfell was a client of West Brooklyn."

"Yes, all right. Wilma writes the letter and then she gets killed. Later Howard Wallace asks you about somebody named Jolene Armbruster. The next day, Howard gets killed. Jolene Armbruster and John Ainsworth have the same initials. Consequently, John Ainsworth has committed welfare fraud and two murders. Is that it?"

"I assure you—" To her annoyance, her voice quavered. She cleared her throat and said more loudly, "I assure you, I don't want it to be true."

Their eyes met across the desk. After a moment, Sunny said with some gentleness, "No, I guess you don't. He's done it to you, too, hasn't he?"

"Oh, certainly." Oddly, the sympathy increased her determination. "As you said, he can't help it; it's just the way he comes on. But," she added grimly, "one makes the effort to keep the mind clear."

Sunny drew a breath and let it out in what was nearly a sigh.

Martha said, "If you'll bear with me, I'd like to play

a little devil's advocate for a few minutes. It's obvious that you know John very well. Putting aside your feeling for him, *could* he have been defrauding the welfare system?''

"Martha Patterson," said Sunny with a lopsided smile, "you are one tough cookie."

It was acquiescence.

Martha said, "He's an actor. He specialized in improvisation. To impersonate Jolene Armbruster as a welfare recipient, he'd have to present himself as a woman."

"I've seen him do it." Sunny had, for the moment at least, taken up the challenge.

"He's very fair. Could he do a black woman?"

"Wig and makeup."

"Mightn't a wig be obvious? And his features are WASP."

Sunny said, "Poor women who wear wigs wear obvious ones. And there are black people with thin lips and narrow noses. A good deal of what we think of as blackness is social. He told me once what creates the illusion is body language and voice."

"The homeless Santa Claus. Yes. All right, let's assume he could. Now, *would* he?"

"Not for the money. Definitely not for the money. But…" Sunny's voice trailed off.

"A challenge to his craft?"

"And maybe a payback."

"Ah."

"Did you know he grew up on welfare?"

"He told me."

"It does things to you."

Martha heard something in her voice. "I'm guessing that you speak from experience."

Sunny said, "You're looking at one of those unwed teenage mothers who are personally responsible for the entire federal deficit. I finally got off when Holly was six. She's thirteen now, and I hope she'll remember just enough to know that what they say about it is bullshit." Sunny drew in a breath and closed her eyes. More quietly, she said, "You channel it, but it's still anger."

"Indeed."

"But…but even if—" She blew out an annoyed breath. "I can't even say it. Try again, Merry Sunshine. OK. Even if John did do something so crazy and stupid as committing welfare fraud, I don't see how Wilma could have found out."

Martha said, "She followed people."

"What do you mean?"

"It seems to have been a sort of compulsion. People would capture her interest and she'd take to following them around. She followed me home from the office." Martha nodded at the photocopy on the desk. "That's how she got my address."

"That's spooky."

"She knew John from seeing him around the office. What if the Ainsworth charm worked on her? Think about it. What if she followed him home and hung around on the street waiting for him to go out and recognized him in the Jolene Armbruster disguise?"

"Martha," said Sunny, "this is ridiculous." She had abandoned the game.

Martha said, "I'd certainly like it to be."

"It is. It's ridiculous. He'd never jeopardize everything like that. Don't you know how much pride he takes in having got to where he is from where he started? My God, Martha, do you know what he's accomplished? Yale summa, Columbia Law, *Law Review,* member of the bar. He wouldn't jeopardize that. Some druggie broke into Wilma's apartment and surprised her.''

''And the letter?''

''Paranoia. Or maybe Carlos. You know why we're doing this, don't you?''

Martha raised her eyebrows.

''We're making him into a villain so we can escape.''

''Escape?''

''That damn magnetism. It's got you, but you don't want to look like a doting old woman, so you're counteracting the attraction by turning him into a villain.''

It was, perhaps, not an entirely outrageous theory. Certainly that twenty-eight-year-old part of Martha responded powerfully to that young man, though she was far from persuaded that she was in danger of behaving as a doting old woman. ''But surely it's appropriate for you,'' she said.

''No, it isn't.''

''Why on earth not?''

''Because,'' said Sunny, ''in my sane moments, I know it isn't going to work. Because I'm responsible to Holly, not to my nerve endings.''

''Your daughter doesn't get along with him?''

''Holly thinks he's wonderful.''

''I don't understand.''

''Right now,'' Sunny said, ''It's OK. He treats her like a pesky little sister. It's easy now; she's thirteen and she's all bones and braces. But someday she's going to be fifteen, and sixteen, and eighteen. When I'm thinking straight, I know it isn't an acceptable risk. But break it off? Those damn nerve endings are in control. So to get off the hook, I'm colluding in this neurotic construct of yours."

TWENTY-NINE

THE BUS was a lurching island of light. Martha thought she must be looking her full age, for someone actually got up and offered her a seat—one of the front seats that she normally disdained, with the decal requesting riders to save them for the elderly and disabled. She accepted this offer.

It was inviting, this notion of Sunny's. There was no denying that a part of Martha responded to John in a manner that, if observed, would invite derision from the world at large. She knew that one of her great fears was appearing foolish. What if she was, after all, demonizing John simply in order to neutralize his attraction?

But there were things she hadn't discussed with Sunny.

John knew about Wilma's search for someone to trust; he had been standing beside Martha in the waiting room when she told Enid. What if he had believed Wilma meant to inform on him? What if he had gone back for the sweatshirt, thinking to use an anonymous black garment to hide himself in the darkness?

The devil made itself black.

He knew Wilma's psychiatric examination was scheduled for that evening; he could have learned that Olivia Ullbright was the assigned psychiatrist. Her telephone was listed; he could have found her address—only a few blocks from where he lived. Anonymous in the black sweatshirt, he could have waited outside for

Wilma and Enid to come out and followed them to McDonald's, followed Wilma home (on the way retrieving the McDonald containers from whatever trash can she had thrown them into—for McInerny was positive she wouldn't have waited to get home before eating). He could have crept up to the fourth floor while she was quarreling with McInerny. The fourth-floor hall light was out; he could have hidden in the shadows and waylaid her as she unlocked her door, the struggle causing the sound "like gym shoes squeakin'" that Tessie had heard. He could have dressed her still-warm body in her nightgown, dumped the McDonald's containers in the garbage can, rumpled the bed, turned on the television, gone out the window and down the fire escape—

A busy night. He hadn't finished the brief. He had come in the next morning saying he had gone off the track—

Howard? Not finding a Jolene Armbruster case in the GBU files, Howard could have asked John about the name—

And Sasquatch and the Loch Ness monster could be cruising in the Bermuda Triangle. This theory made about as much sense. Olivia Ullbright thought Wilma had been expecting a windfall; in the absence of a secret legacy, Martha had thought of blackmail. But blackmail is the price of silence; if Wilma had meant to blackmail a perpetrator of welfare fraud, she would not have been looking for someone in whom to confide her suspicions.

A clear head would note that the source of the nonsense was surely Wilma herself. The windfall and the thefts from the "system" were very likely elements of the active fantasy life Olivia Ullbright had observed.

Burglaries occurred around the clock in this city; the resulting deaths of two acquaintances within a week constituted no more than a striking coincidence.

She would tell that sharp man, Detective Sharpman, about Jolene Armbruster. She would finish her departure memo, make her court appearance in the morning, and go on to whatever came next.

IT WAS a quarter to six when the bus let Martha off half a block from West Brooklyn. She wondered at the wisdom of entering the office after hours, but she could see lighted windows on the fourth floor. She wouldn't be alone.

In the corner office, the sight of Luther Young sitting at the director's desk still set off a little shock wave. But the frown furrows between his brows were less deep than usual, and when he said, "Oh, Ms. Patterson, I thought you'd left," his bass rumble was almost cordial.

"I had an appointment out of the office," said Martha. "Do you plan to stay much longer?"

He glanced up at the wall clock. "About an hour."

"I'd appreciate it if you'd let me know when you're leaving. I'm not prepared to stay here alone."

He nodded. "Very wise."

Heading back, she caught herself glancing into John's office; her stomach lurched as she realized how habitual that glance had become. He looked up as she passed and said, "Hi, Martha." His eyes were dark-circled and lines once more showed around his mouth.

What if Sunny had picked up her phone as soon as Martha had left, to warn John about this doting old woman's neurotic construct?

She said, "Hello, John," and went on. Three doors

farther along, Victory King looked up and said, "Hi, Martha."

Oh, there was much in this place that she would miss.

In her own office, she shrugged out of her coat and flung it across the client chair—in which no more clients would sit. She was about a third of the way through her memo when John appeared in her doorway. "Luther and I are leaving," he said. "He said you wanted to know."

Even under Luther Young's escort, Martha didn't intend to accompany John anywhere. "Is anybody else here?" she asked.

"A couple in L and T, and Enid may still be back in Family Law."

"Thank you. I'll stay on until they go."

"I'll tell them you're here. Don't stay alone."

She forced a smile. "I have no intention of doing so." She pushed her chair back. "I'll tell them myself, in fact."

The couple in Landlord-Tenant turned out to be truly a couple—a male and a female lounging in an office, coffee mugs in hand and a fifth of Scotch on the desk. They offered Martha a shot, which she declined on the ground that finishing her memo required a clear head. They promised to collect her when they left.

She had finished four more case summaries when Enid Morgan put her head in the door and said, "Sorry to bother you. Do you still have Wilma's file?"

"I'm afraid I do." Martha rummaged. "I should have returned it to you." She moved one legal pad and uncovered another. It was the pad on which she had originally started her departure memo; she saw "Jolene Armbruster" scrawled across the middle of the sheet and, irritated with these recurrent jolts to the solar plexus, turned it facedown.

Enid reached out and turned it back over. "Where'd you get that name?" she asked.

Martha was going to carry on no more conversations about Jolene Armbruster with anyone but Detective Sharpman. "I don't know. It popped into my head and I wrote it down so that in case I turn out to need it, I won't have forgotten it again." She rummaged further and uncovered Wilma's file.

Enid took it. "Are we the last ones here?"

"There are a couple of people in Landlord-Tenant having Happy Hour with a fifth of Scotch," said Martha.

"Oh, that'll be Debbie and Morris. Before Howard, it was pot. I guess I'll go around and let them make me an offer I can't refuse."

But she returned after a moment. "No luck. They're gone."

Annoyed, Martha said, "They promised they'd tell me when they were leaving."

"Other things on their minds."

"No doubt. So we are the last, after all."

"Looks like it. Don't you go without telling me."

Martha looked at her list. Four more cases to do. "This place gives me goose bumps," she said. "Why don't we go now? I can finish in the morning."

Enid said, "Give me ten minutes."

IN FACT, it was closer to twenty minutes before Enid reappeared. She had changed into navy blue sweats; running shoes and sweat socks replaced her pumps; a waist pack replaced her handbag. She set a gym bag on the floor and came into the office while Martha got up from her desk and slipped the file for tomorrow's court appearance into her briefcase.

The space was so tiny that two people crowded it. When Martha bent to take her handbag from the bottom desk drawer, her backside bumped Enid's thighs. "I beg your pardon," she said, but Enid did not move. Straightening with handbag in hand, Martha found the full length of her back against Enid's body.

For a moment she wondered if she was experiencing a lesbian advance. But when she heard Enid's shoe soles squeak on the floor tiles, Tessie's "basketball game" flashed across her mind and her inner eye saw Detective Jamison replay the choke hold that had killed Wilma Oberfell.

Enid?

Her handbag hit the floor as she flung her right arm up. She just intercepted the arm snaking around her neck. She flung her head backward and felt a crunch as the back of her skull smashed into Enid's face. Her free hand clawed at the arm around her neck and found the hand; she shifted her weight onto one leg and kicked backward with the other and felt her heel catch Enid's shin. She scraped her shoe sole down and stamped with all her weight on Enid's instep while her fingers closed on a thumb and wrenched outward.

The pressure on her neck slackened. She banged her head backward again, jerked the thumb again, and tore free of the armlock.

The struggle had shifted their positions; now the office door was in front of Martha. Moving faster than she had done in twenty years, she clattered into the corridor, turned right to the back stairs, wrenched at the knob, and leaned her full weight on the door. It opened; she staggered into the stairwell, clutched the rail, and raced downward. The door latched behind her.

Her solitary attempts to replicate the maneuvers in the self-defense book had not been as futile as she had thought.

She was past the between-floors landing before she heard the door open above; she was nearly down to the third floor before she heard the thump of running shoes hitting the concrete steps over her head. She swung past the closed fire door. The faster rhythm of Enid's running feet made a crazy counterpoint with her jarring steps. Around the next landing, down again. Enid was just swinging around on the landing above as Martha reached the second floor.

The fire door was open, propped with a wedge.

Could somebody still be in the building?

She shoved the door back, kicked the wedge out of the way, and bolted through into a dark corridor. The door swung ponderously closed behind her.

It was a public corridor, lined with office doors. Her panicky glance picked up no lights showing through their frosted glass, but thirty feet along a red exit sign glowed overhead. She ran, heard noise behind her, risked a quick glance. The back-stairs door was opening.

But she had reached the exit. Again she wrenched open a fire door and bolted into a stairwell, plunged down again, and swung around the landing. On the last half-flight, her right foot slipped and her left foot came down crazily on the edge of a step. Only her grip on the stair rail saved her, and now each step was an agony to her twisted ankle. But she reached the door at the ground floor and shoved through into the deep alcove that extended along the side of the elevator shaft, hobbled into the lobby, and flung herself against the heavy glass front doors.

They didn't give.

Behind her, the stairway doorknob rattled. Both elevators stood open and lighted. As she turned, her twisted ankle gave way and she fell to her hands and knees. She scrambled backward on all fours, tumbled across the nearest elevator-door track, clawed herself to her knees, and punched the nearest button with her left hand. The elevator door rumbled and began to move.

But Enid had only to come around the corner and slap the edge of the closing door to send it open again.

The door slid; the space shrank—

Enid came into view. Blood was trickling from her nose down her chin, black streaks soaking the navy of her sweatshirt. Her eyes turned left, right, spotted the closing elevator door. She plunged forward, her hand stretched toward the narrowing slit. But she was just too far away; her hand hit the flat of the door short of the edge.

The slit closed. The elevator lurched and began to sink. The lobby floor rose sluggishly past the little square window in the door.

Martha was safe.

But it would open again in the basement. She scrambled to her knees and reached for the control panel. Her groping fingers found the on-off switch, and forced it up—

CLANGANGANGANG—

It was a moment before she realized that the switch had activated an alarm. She was half deafened, but the elevator had stopped, sheltering her between floors.

Enid. Good God.

—CLANGANGANGANG—

THIRTY

Oh, my God,'' said John. ''Yes, I must have. I used my own initials a lot for improv, so I'm sure I did for the role-play.''

It was seven o'clock Friday evening. They were in Martha's apartment. The chaise accommodated her walking cast; Sunny and John shared the facing sofa.

The elevator alarm, Martha had learned, was connected to the precinct house. Presently she had heard police officers shouting down the shaft over the din. They had to send an officer to the basement before she was willing to turn the switch to on. She talked to Detective Sharpman in the emergency room. The police found her briefcase beside her handbag on the floor of her office; Luther persuaded them to release the file inside; in the morning John answered the calendar call and successfully argued the case. That evening he brought her the news, along with her handbag, her briefcase, an African violet, and Sunny.

''Did Howard ask you about the name?'' asked Martha.

''Just if I'd ever had a client with that name. I hadn't, and that was as far as it went. My mind was on the argument in the Eastern District. God, if I'd remembered, Howard would still be alive.''

''I doubt,'' said Martha, ''if remembering that you used the name Jolene Armbruster in a conference role-play would lead one inevitably to the conclusion that

Enid used it three years later to defraud the Department of Social Services.''

''Well, she was there,'' John said. ''She was at that damn conference because I talked her into it, and she was in the bar with me when that idiot woman was running off at the mouth. I might have remembered that.''

''John, don't wallow,'' said Sunny. ''Memory's a chancy thing. I blanked her out, too.''

John said, ''When she was a kid, she got paid for taking the garbage out, so she sneaked in junk from the street to make more loads. She wrote papers for guys she tutored in college. Once somebody paid her to take half the bar exam. She called it taking care of herself. I should have thought of that when Wilma came in saying she didn't trust anybody.''

''Howard must have asked her about the name,'' said Martha. ''An hour or two before the board meeting, he came by while I was talking with her and asked to see her. I suppose he thought Wilma might have mentioned Jolene Armbruster to her lawyer.''

''So she got her damn gun and shot him.''

Sunny said, ''What if I'd known about Jolene Armbruster? What if I'd run into her somewhere and mentioned the name?''

''Oh, my God,'' said John.

ENID HAD BEEN arrested as she returned from a run. She attributed her broken nose and dislocated thumb to a fall. A search of trash baskets along her route turned up an unregistered handgun, a natural-hair Negroid wig, and the scissored fragments of Jolene Armbruster's welfare ID card. Forensic tests matched the gun's bullets to those removed from Howard's body, matched the wig to the hair found in the sweatshirt, and established the patched-together photo on the ID card as a portrait of Enid in dark makeup and probably the same wig.

A CALL FROM SUNNY was waiting on Martha's answering machine when she returned from Christmas in California. Congress was contemplating severe cuts in the Legal Services budget, possibly outright defunding. West Brooklyn was already strapped. Would Martha be interested in volunteering a day or two a week at WAO to advise clients of their legal rights?

Part-time proved to be quite stimulating enough.

THE WELFARE inspector general tracked "Jolene Armbruster" through the system to the assistant office manager in the Bronx, who admitted to creating twenty fictional cases and named Enid Morgan as one of her outside confederates. For three years "Jolene Armbruster" had received an AFDC grant for herself and five mythical children; a second case had been opened a few months later. Even after splitting with the AOM, Enid had enjoyed an annual tax-free salary supplement of over ten thousand dollars, not to mention thousands of dollars in food stamps, which perhaps she had spent or perhaps had sold on the black market.

The assistant district attorney prosecuting the cases told Martha that a cashier at a check-cashing office remembered an obese blond woman coming in shortly after Thanksgiving, showing a DSS employee's ID card, and asking for the name of somebody who had just been in. He tentatively identified Wilma from a snapshot in Geraldine's possession and "Jolene Armbruster" from the reconstructed ID photo. Neither Tessie Doone nor Francis McInerny, however, was able to pick Enid out of a lineup of tall, wigged, sweatshirted women as the hooded figure on the stairs and the fire escape.

An investigator who was "good with loony-tunes" had several conversations with Madonna (whose name proved to be Ellen Blaustock). Madonna had seen "the light one" eating her Big Mac and fries while talking to "the dark one" on the bench in the middle of Broadway. The dark one later took the light one's containers from the trash basket where she had placed them.

"Will Madonna testify?" asked Martha.

"Jesus," said the ADA.

OLIVIA ULLBRIGHT remembered that Enid had a gym bag with her that night.

"What's going to happen to Carlos Quinones?" asked Martha.

"Nothing," said the ADA. "He's cooperating and the head of the office isn't pressing charges."

"What about his kneecaps?"

"He's studying karate."

GWEN DOHERTY telephoned in February. "John said you'd like to hear that Tessie won her hearing."

"Congratulations," said Martha. "Did you get the retroactive as well?"

"The whole ball of wax. We put in the affidavit, and the ALJ decided she had successfully rebutted the presumption, blah blah blah, grant to be restored retroactively to the date of discontinuance."

"Was there any problem about where the money came from?"

"Never came up."

"How is Kareem doing? Is he in college?"

"Last I heard he was, but Kareem's out of there. He moved in with the girlfriend."

THE ADA pieced together the scraps and proposed the following set of conjectures:

When Enid was assigned to her case, Wilma started following her around and eventually spotted her in the Jolene Armbruster disguise. On the fatal Monday, Wilma also followed Carlos from The Building to the loan shark's office to the crowded corridors of housing court, where she overheard him tell Luther he had been mugged.

The two episodes together so outraged Wilma that she came looking for the "one in charge" to inform on both of them. Failing in that attempt, she wrote the letters and left them in McInerny's apartment, intending to buy stamps and mail them the next day. When the psychiatrist questioned her ability to support Rosemary, however, Wilma changed her mind and decided to blackmail Enid.

Meanwhile, disturbed by Martha's news about Wilma's visit to the office, Enid began to entertain the notion of silencing her client. She pinched the office sweatshirt, picked up the Jolene Armbruster wig at home, and carried them to Olivia Ullbright's office in her gym bag. The conversation Madonna witnessed outside McDonald's was probably Wilma's effort to open blackmail negotiations. This development converted Enid's notion into a decision. She retrieved Wilma's garbage and stashed it in her gym bag with the idea of using it to confuse the time of death, then went around the corner and put on the wig and sweatshirt.

The devil made itself black.

"Why did she use the office sweatshirt?" Martha asked. "It just turned the investigation back to West Brooklyn."

"Damned if I know," said the ADA. "I don't know what she expected to get out of messing with the time of death, either. I'd say she was rattled from the minute she heard Oberfell had been in the office."

THEY NEVER found Wilma's letter to Howard.

THE DISTRICT ATTORNEY obtained indictments for, in ascending order of difficulty, welfare fraud, attempt to commit murder in the second degree, and two counts of murder in the second degree. Enid pleaded guilty to the first and, in spite of her claim that she had left the office to go running while Martha was still there, was rather quickly found guilty of the second. Both murder juries, on the other hand, struggled with the conjectures for days until, in each case, a mistrial was declared. A new DA, elected in November, looked at the evidence, listened to Madonna, and declined to use any more of her office's resources to prepare for retrials. Enid would be eligible to apply for parole in a little over eight years.

IN JANUARY, a year and a month after she left West Brooklyn Legal Services, Martha returned with aching knees, a sore ankle, and refreshed spirit from a cross-country weekend and discovered in her mailbox an envelope with Carlos Quinones's return address. Settled on the chaise with a cup of tea, she opened it and found a letter folded around a bundle of currency: four fifties, a ten, and two singles.

Dear Martha [she read],

The eighth step says we should make a list of all persons we harmed and become willing to make amends to them all, and the ninth step says we should make amends to them wherever possible except when to do so would injure them or others. That's the exact words.

Your name was way up on my list, but driving a cab, it took a while. Here's the money that was in your wallet, the best I can remember how much it was. They aren't kidding when they say our lives had become unmanageable.

I hope things are going good for you. I'm hanging in. I was talking to Luther about maybe getting taken back at West Brooklyn, but there's budget problems. There isn't any other work that really grabs me. Even though you were only there a couple of weeks, and got an extremely raw deal, getting ripped off and fired and half strangled, I sort of think you know what I mean.

Sincerely yours,
Carlos Quinones

BONES

JOHN PAXSON

A MONTANA MYSTERY

Former journalist Ben Tripp does a bit of small-time
private investigating. Mostly stray dogs, straying
husbands and general snooping around the
Bitterroot Valley of western Montana.
Pretty tame stuff until now.

Scott Grady, a paleontology student, is missing,
and a gorgeous professor hires Tripp to do some
digging. As Tripp sifts his way through the cutthroat
world of academia, he uncovers more than Grady's
bones; he digs up the mother lode of motives...and
a killer who staked his claim.

Available March 1999 at your favorite retail outlet.

MURDER AT THE MOVIES

CHARLENE WEIR
GEORGE BAXT
MAXINE O'CALLAGHAN

MURDER TAKE TWO
by Charlene Weir

Hollywood comes to Hampstead, Kansas, with the filming of a new picture starring sexy actress Laura Edwards. But murder steals the scene when a stunt double is impaled on a pitchfork.

THE HUMPHREY BOGART MURDER CASE
by George Baxt

Hollywood in its heyday is brought to life in this witty caper featuring a surprise sleuth—Humphrey Bogart. While filming *The Maltese Falcon*, he searches for a real-life treasure, dodging a killer on a murder trail through Hollywood.

SOMEWHERE SOUTH OF MELROSE
by Maxine O'Callaghan

P.I. Delilah West is hired to search for an old high school classmate. The path takes her through the underbelly of broken dreams and into the caprices of fate, where secrets are born and sometimes kept....

Available March 1999 at your favorite retail outlet.

Look us up on-line at: http://www.worldwidemystery.com   WMOM305